Oh, Louisa!

Oh, Louisa!

Historical Fiction

Becca Anderson

Oh, Louisa!

Cover Design: Becca Anderson. Materials from Freepik.com, images 10393868, 5377, 2148950962. Back cover photo from *Yankee Magazine*, January 1971 issue.

ISBN: 978-0-9995880-1-7

Oh, Louisa! Is a work of fiction based on history. References to real people, events, establishments, organizations, or locales are true as researched, but are intended only to provide a sense of authenticity and are used ficticiously. Some characters, incidents, and dialogue are drawn from the author's imagination. See Author's Notes for details.

Printed in the U.S.A.

TO
MARCIA REED TODD,
my mother, whose 100th birthday was the
push I needed to finish this book

AND TO
WILMA CARR,
the best first reader a writer could have

AND ESPECIALLY TO
LOUISA JANE HOVEY DESASSEVILLE
who lived a life worth writing about

TABLE OF CONTENTS

Part 1

Prologue

Spring, 1881, Boston

The chalk left a dusty trail of information across the blackboard as Louisa surreptitiously glanced at the image reflected in the picture frame glass above the board.

"Back in your seat, young man, or I'll tie you to the desk."

The boy froze midstep, newly convinced his teacher had eyes in the back of her head and slumped onto his bench. The boys around him snickered, elbowing each other in delight. With his pranks and teasing, he was the bane of their existence.

"Now, who can tell me what Manifest Destiny means?" Louisa tried to rub the dry chalk dust from her fingers as she faced the class again. Eighteen pairs of eyes dropped to desktops, feet shuffled, and silence descended. "Anyone?"

With a sigh, Louisa put one hand on an ample hip and prepared to call on one of her students. Surprisingly, the class troublemaker Guy Holiday piped up.

"It's what they talk about in the papers all the time," he said, frowning. "But I don't get it."

A small smile creased Louisa's heavy features. "At least one of you is honest enough to admit your ignorance. Manifest Destiny is the idea that our country should grow from the East Coast to the

West Coast and include all that land as part of our nation. There's so much more to this country than just the cities and farms of the East!"

The boys locked their eyes on their teacher. Her enthusiasm was plain, and it carried them along. They also knew that if they kept her on this subject long enough, the class period would elapse, and they could go outside to joyfully burn off some young boy energy.

A hand went up from the back of the class. Louisa nodded. "Yes, Henry?"

"Ma'am, my dad says nobody in their right mind would want to go west when everything we need is in the East." He crossed his arms just as Louisa had seen his father do many times and sat back. The rest of the class also relaxed; the gauntlet had been thrown down, and their teacher was bound to pick it up.

"I would never want to contradict your father, Henry, but maybe he doesn't know enough about the West to understand what it offers," she said carefully. "Yes, we have cities, farms, railroads, the seat of government, and great ports here in the East. But is that all we need?" She paused, one eyebrow rising in excitement.

"What about breathing space? Grand vistas of snow-capped peaks soaring into the sky? Great herds of buffalo and antelope thundering across the plains? Adventures around every corner and characters who seem like they just walked out of the pages of books on every hill?"

Her heart began to speed, her eyes flashed, and Louisa's vision drifted to the imagined grandeur of what she was describing. Her small life as a maiden schoolteacher moving through her late thirties shrank to insignificance. She had her tidy room in her half-sister Rebecca's comfortable Boston home, the clockwork precision of Rebecca's husband George's comings and goings, and the prim censorship of George's mother Elizabeth, her small circle of similar friends, her cocoon of predictability.

Henry snorted. "Says who? I think they made it all up."

Louisa turned slowly to the boy, focusing on his pugnacious scowl. "Well," she said, her voice soft and dreamy, "maybe you just have to go see for yourself."

As the boys ran boisterously outside the window of the teacher's lounge, Louisa brooded over her cup of tea. Her childhood friend and fellow teacher, Harriet Davenport, studied her with concern.

"Bad day, Louisa? That mop-headed boy get your goat again?" She chuckled, trying to lift her friend's spirits. But Louisa just sighed.

"I think I'm a fraud, Harriet." She shook her head and took a sip of the tea. "I stand up in front of those boys and talk about things I only read in books. But am I right about them? What if everything I'm saying is something somebody told somebody, and it's all twisted out of proportion? What if I'm not telling them the truth?"

"Oh, my. That's a heavy thought. We're teachers. That's what we do; we tell them what we've learned from others who learned it from still others."

"And if they are wrong?"

Harriet laughed. "Then I suppose we just perpetuate the errors. But will it change anybody's life if we don't get it perfectly right?" She tapped the back of Louisa's plump hand with a long finger. "What's really behind this?"

A small smile flitted across Louisa's face, moving her big cheeks slightly. A lock of her already-graying hair flopped over her left ear, and she firmly patted it back. "It's the West. We got on the subject today, and I suddenly realized I talk about it all the time and have no idea what it's like. Yet it dominates our social consciousness," she paused. "It dominates *my* mind, too."

Harriet leaned in. "If you were a man, you could hop a train and see it yourself." She closed her eyes. "Oh, to be brave and free like that."

3

Louisa locked her eyes on Harriet's face. "Maybe you don't have to be a man to be brave. Maybe freedom comes because you grab it. Maybe I'm braver and freer than I think." She rose and crossed the lounge with decisive steps as the recess bell sounded. She put her cup and saucer on the serving tray on the way out. Harriet tilted her head and watched her, then shook it in amused affection.

CHAPTER 1

July, 1881

Louisa shifted in the too-upright train seat to ease an ache in her shoulder. She resumed her reading of *Harper's Weekly*, studying the drawing of a projection of New York City in the coming years. The towering wall of buildings looming over the harbor made the ships look like toys.

"Imagine!" she murmured. "What will it be like to go to the top?" Then she recalled when she arrived, the soaring Rocky Mountains would dwarf even those massive structures.

She folded the magazine thoughtfully and put it in her travel bag. She'd save the rest of it for the morning. This night train from Chicago to Cheyenne capped a busy and tiring day. Her eyes drifted shut, and the train rocked. She let her mind drift to the preparations she'd made over the course of a month to make the trip possible. The voices of her family and friends still rang in her ears.

"You're going where?? Oh, Louisa, do be serious. I forbid you to go." Her brother Charles' eyebrows formed a rigid line across his forehead, and his generous mustache bristled with disapproval.

"Oh, do you think it's quite safe? What about Indians?" Her half-sister Rebecca's soft voice and worried brown eyes caused her to sigh.

"You're going! I knew you would someday!" Harriet Davenport, a regular invitee for Sunday dinner, enthused. When family members turned their stern faces toward her, she ignored them and focused on Louisa's twinkling eyes. "I wish I could go with you."

The mustache twitched again. "I will not pay for such a frivolous and ridiculous expedition." If Charles were still carrying his sword from the war, without doubt, he'd have been rattling it. The glint in his eye gave his younger sister a small inkling of what his foes had seen across the battlefields of Antietam and Gettysburg.

Louisa shook her head and took a sip of wine. "I don't recall asking you to pay for it. Thanks to what Father left me and my teaching salary, I have the money I need and more. I plan to travel as inexpensively as is realistic and yet to have enough to bring back a souvenir to remind me of my adventure."

"That money is for your old age! I won't let you spend it."

"Then I'm glad it is beyond your control. Charles, I'm 41 years old. I'm not a child under your roof. I didn't bring this subject up to fluster you or irritate anyone. Or to ask permission. I am merely letting you know my plans for the summer."

"In my day, a woman stayed home," Rebecca's mother-in-law said with a sniff. "You have a lovely room here and leisure time to spare. Why do you have to do something so silly?"

Louisa correctly placed her fork and knife at the top of the plate to signal she had finished her meal, folded her napkin, and looked at them all as the silence drew out. Servants cleared the plates, and the men moved to George's den for cigars and whiskey—and, no doubt, more outraged talk.

The women rose to adjourn to the parlor and their needlepoint. Louise-Caroline, Charles' wife, took the opportunity to hold her sister-in-law back for a moment.

"My dear, don't listen to them. You go see your beloved West. You know they're just jealous of your courage. Then you come home and tell me all about it. I can't wait to hear it." Later, Louise-Caroline had pressed some money into Louisa's hand and told her to put it toward a gift for herself in Denver. Her warm embrace was all the affirmation Louisa needed. Her sister-in-law would douse Charles' fire while she was away.

Louisa's half-sleeping mind drifted to days of packing, purchasing train tickets, and planning itineraries. She kept careful records of each expense and made notes in a small book of details she wanted to remember. At last, the morning of her departure dawned, and she stood on the train platform waiting for an express to Albany. Her only companions were Harriet and Louise-Caroline since her other relatives refused to sanction her plan or even wish her a safe journey.

"Be well, be excited, be inquisitive," Harriet enthused. "Soak it in and then come back with wild and woolly tales. I'm proud of you."

Louise-Caroline embraced her, and her soft scent of lavender left a home-like comfort on Louisa's clothing. "You are the strongest and best of us all. We'll be here when you get home."

When the whistle blew, and the train entered the station, a porter transferred Louisa's trunk to the baggage car, and another helped her aboard. She waved from the window and took the first deep breath she'd been able to manage in weeks. She wondered how the air would smell in Denver.

Now, here she was, leaving Chicago and heading West on the Union Pacific, joining up with the new Transcontinental Railroad. From Cheyenne, she would take the branch line to her final destination. Excitement crackled through her, making her eyes dart back and forth behind her closed lids. She let go of conscious thought and drifted to sleep to the clacking of the railway and the snores of fellow passengers.

CHAPTER 2

July 1881, Denver

S he wasn't sure whether the air's thinness or the soaring
mountains' magnificence made it hard to breathe. Louisa
stood transfixed by the enormity of the Rockies. Though she'd been
gazing at them from the train windows for many hours, they
seemed more prominent and weightier without the thin glass
barrier between them. She finally understood what it was like to fall
in love.

Fellow passengers retrieved their luggage, called for porters,
and greeted friends and loved ones. She was oblivious. She thought
she'd never need to eat or drink again if she could drink in the view
deeply enough. But eventually, the hovering porter at her elbow
made an impression on her, and she tore her eyes away from the
sublime to the mundane once more.

"Yes, just this bag and the trunk there," she said, gesturing to the
hump-backed container she'd borrowed from Louise-Caroline to
the teeth-grinding indignation of her brother Charles. I want to go
to the Windsor Hotel." The porter tipped his hat and began
organizing her trunk and horse-drawn cab. Everything was noise,
color, and foreign smells. It exhilarated her.

As her cab jounced over the rough roads to the hotel, Louisa tried to capture as many sights and sounds as possible in preparation for her next letter to Harriet. She thought of the words she could write to make clear that the entire city seemed to be electric with activity—but not the kind she'd experienced in Boston or New York City. There were no orderly gatherings of men in suits but shopkeepers, men from the mining fields, women and children hurrying to and fro, and a din of horses, shouts, and construction. Everywhere she looked, construction.

The trip was only a matter of blocks, and if she'd known the way and could manage her trunk, she would have walked to the hotel to better absorb everything. She pledged to explore on foot as much as possible during her stay.

A doorman retrieved her trunk from the cab as she stepped under the iron *porte-cochere* to the Ladies' Entrance. The five-story castle, built to resemble Windsor Castle in England, sported American and Union Jack flags. A breeze lifted her collar and her spirits, and she smiled broadly.

Her name in the register made her feel she'd finally arrived in Denver. Everywhere she looked, adventure wooed her to explore.

One of the smaller rooms in the hotel would comfortably accommodate her. She had read there were 400 rooms, some as conservative as hers and some palatial suites for the wealthy. Louisa wasn't there for the hotel; she was there for Denver and the West. Her room offered a view across rooftops to the snow-capped peaks beyond.

What to do first? Louisa dithered as the maid efficiently unpacked her trunk and stored her clothes in the wardrobe and dresser. A nap would be lovely. The crisp air outside called her when she opened the window. The rumble of activity in the street stirred her feet to join it. She forced herself to sit at the small desk and take out some stationery and a pen.

Dearest Harriet,

I can hardly believe I am writing these words: I have arrived in Denver! Before I explore, I am sending you a note letting you know I am safe and sound. The train journey was a revelation. This country is so big, and so much of it is empty. After the tight streets of Boston, it was like crossing a different planet to see the prairies and the mountains.

Oh, the mountains. I will have much to write about them later. Nothing prepared me for my heart pounding when I first glimpsed them. To have them hovering to the west of Denver, almost leaning over it to watch it grow, is incomparable. They are everything I dreamed of and yet so much more. I plan to get closer to them during this trip.

Denver is raw yet refined. It is bustling with action, all of it seemingly random, but buildings are going up almost as one watches. Workmen of every stripe are on the move, and they are putting up things like this wonderful hotel. It's only been open for a year, but it looks as solid as if it has been here for much longer.

I have splurged on the best hotel in the city for my first night. I will decide later if I want to move to somewhere less expensive for the remainder of my stay. The dining room is breathtaking, as is the menu. I will thoroughly enjoy that tonight. I understand this hotel has a gambling hall, but I will stay far from it. Sadly, there is a steep stairway leading to the worst of the gambling rooms called the Suicide Stairway. Many a broken man has climbed the staircase, I read, only to come down it much more precipitously after losing a fortune.

Shops are accessible down a hallway in the lobby. Can you imagine? My small bedroom has a marble fireplace and everything I need for basic comfort. A bath down the hall is nicely appointed. I could have paid more for a private bath, but I'd rather hoard my funds for more exciting adventures than to wash my face.

My best course of action is to sit here by this sunny window and review my travel guides and maps for the afternoon. Tomorrow, I can venture out refreshed and with a plan for exploration. It feels like anything is possible in this place.

Affectionately,
Louisa

CHAPTER 3

July 1881, Denver

Louisa was glad she had dressed so carefully for her first dinner at the hotel. Elegant people in stylish clothing filled the dining room. The entire scene could have easily been picked up from New York City and dropped in Denver. Candles and chandeliers twinkled, and fine linen cloths were starched stiff enough to stand on their own. Silent, handsome waiters glided from table to table, bringing amazing dishes to tempt any palate.

Waiters silently rolled each course of the meal to the table and served it with a flourish and a smile. Mock Turtle Soup preceded an exquisite Baked Flounder a la Chambord. Roman Punch brought out the sweet and tart flavor of Charlotte Russe for dessert. Dark, rich coffee melted the sugar in her mouth, leaving her feeling delighted.

Her small table at the edge of the dining room, shaded by a wall of potted palms, afforded Louisa plenty of opportunity to watch people in other parts of the room. Women with dancing feathers protruding from their up-swept hair lifted elegant, long-gloved arms to gesture. Their suave escorts exuded well-being and success, from their shined shoes to their gilded watch chains.

Louisa kept her posture correct and affected an air of confidence. She'd long ago learned that people only knew you weren't of their class if you showed them you weren't. She might be a school teacher on a summer holiday, but she had every right to dine in the same style as the upper crust of Denver.

A waiter eased back her chair as she moved to rise, fully satisfied with the meal and the ambiance. "There is dancing in the ballroom this evening if madam would care to partake," he said, gesturing toward the music she had heard throughout dinner.

Intrigued, she nodded and thanked him. The mixed scents of decadent food and rich perfumes from the tables she passed made her turn the opposite way from the ballroom when she saw an outdoor walkway lit by torches. She inhaled deeply, already composing her next letter to Harriet.

Back inside the hotel lobby, Louisa heard a particularly lovely waltz playing. She drifted to the ballroom's doorway to hear the music better. The lights were lower here than in the dining room, and couples spun in lazy sweeps to the lilting violins.

"Have you tried the floating dance floor?" a baritone voice at her elbow drew Louisa's attention. "It's like nothing you've ever experienced before." He gestured to cables connecting the dance area's corners to the ceiling, forming a platform. "I would be honored if you join me for a dance. My name is Rudolpho."

Momentarily taken aback, Louisa took stock of the good-looking owner of the liquid voice. His finely cut tuxedo bracketed a white shirt and gold stick pin in a grey cravat. He bowed slightly and held out a hand. She realized he was one of the paid dance partners of the hotel and gave him a tentative smile. "Louisa," she said, then embraced the moment and took his hand. "I'd love to."

~ ~ ~

Dear Harriet,

I am having an amazing time. My feet are tired from dancing (can you imagine?) I feasted on food I only read about in books.

The American Plan includes my meals, and I have been delighted so far. I chose Baked Flounder a la Chambord. I was not sure what to expect, but it is a lovely piece of fish with skewers of crayfish and mushrooms and pinwheels of white fish, truffles, and caviar. I will never forget the taste of it.

My head is buzzing because I had two glasses of Roman Punch. It was elegantly served in a stemmed glass and included lemonade, orange juice, and champagne, with a whipped concoction of egg whites and confectioner's sugar on top. One was just not enough.

I also enjoyed Charlotte Russe. Have you had it? It consists of layers of ladyfingers and Bavarian cream interspersed (in this case) with tart hot-house strawberries. I admit I had to step outside for air after all that!

This hotel has what is called a floating dance floor. Picture it if you can: a black-and-white checked floor of exotic woods suspended from the ceiling by large cables. As one dances, the floor bounces just slightly and sways. It is accessed via small bridges around the room. My feet would have been even more tired had it not been for this construction, as it was quite pleasant to dance on.

And where did I find a partner? We both can agree I'm not exactly the belle of any ball. But the hotel provides the most handsome men to partner single ladies (or ladies whose husbands do not care to dance or have gone off the gamble), and Rudolpho escorted me throughout the evening. His witting comments and charming looks sent me back to my room on a cloud of enjoyment.

Now I can reseal this envelope, take myself off to bed, and begin my first full day in Denver tomorrow with a tour of the fashionable areas in a handsome cab. I have no regrets coming here.

Louisa

CHAPTER 4

July 1881, Denver

Louisa exited the hotel and stepped smartly along the street, intent on exploring the immediate neighborhood. Her bag held a shawl, lest she became cold, an apple from the breakfast buffet, and her maps and guidebooks. Her face beamed.

My first walk in Denver. My first day to freely wander in a new and intriguing place. I should have done this years ago," she whispered to herself. The rattle of passing coaches stirred puffs of dust in the street, but the crisp air seemed to whisk them away before they could bother her. The sun peeped between the buildings, and she could hear the whistle of trains arriving at Union Station, a few blocks away.

When she came to a park where she could see to the west and enjoy the shade of fragrant pines, she sought a bench and lowered herself in happy silence. *Her mountains*, as she thought of them, caught the morning sun with their white snowy hats and craggy faces. She would find out how to take a tour to put her in their shadow while she was out today. It would be the ultimate treat of her trip.

Despite the peace of the small park, noises from the busy streets around her drew Louisa back to her feet. She marveled at the steady industry she saw all around her as she walked. Wagons loaded with goods for the mines jounced past, their mule teams flicking at persistent flies. Men hammered at building sites, raising the frames of homes and other structures.

People stepped on and off the wooden boardwalks to avoid porters carrying loads or other people stepping out of doors bordering the street. A rough man on horseback clothed completely in dingy, stained buckskins, a bedroll behind his saddle, and a rifle at the ready stuck in a holder at his knee, moved slowly down the street. His droopy mustache and long, unwashed hair under a sagging hat framed a face disgusted by all the activity that captivated her.

The Boston accent caught her ear after she'd walked for over an hour, and she turned her head. A cab had stopped at the side of the street, and a man climbed down and handed the cabby his fare.

"Thank you, sir. Have a pleasant day," he said with a tip of his cap. The customer nodded, gripped his satchel, and entered an office building. The cabby looked about him for another fare, then removed his hat and wiped his forehead. He took out a pipe and began to fill it.

The scent of the pipe, so like her father's, and his squashed Boston vowels decided Louisa. She looked both ways to avoid other people and stepped up to the cab.

"Excuse me, I would like to ride around the city. Do you do that kind of thing?"

"Yes, ma'am." He climbed down, preparing to assist her into the open chaise. "Anywhere in particular you want to go?"

"I'm visiting from Boston. Honestly, your accent drew me to your cab. I would like to ride around and see whatever you think I would find interesting."

"Boston! What part?" the cabby cried out.

"Roxbury."

"I know it! It's been years since I've been there, but I'm sure it's the same."

"Nothing much changes there, you're right," Louisa sighed. "So, will you drive me around? What will it cost?"

16

"How long do you want to ride?"

"A couple of hours, I think. Are you willing?"

"Course." He helped Louisa step up, saw her properly settled, and then climbed back to his seat. "I know just the places to go. What if we say five cents? It's nice to have home folk to drive around."

"That would be perfect," Louisa said, placing her bag at her feet.

A gentle reins snap urged the horse into motion, and Louisa relaxed in the seat. She could see the action around her from the higher vantage of the cab and not worry about being bumped or jostled or constantly having to watch her feet to avoid the inevitable leftovers of the mule teams. They headed east and turned south along Grant Street as the cabby kept a running commentary.

"I came here chasing the gold like lots of men but figured out pretty quickly it was a lot easier to take gold coins from customers than go grubbing in the mountains looking for flakes of it. My daddy was a cabby in Boston and I figured I could do the same here. Of course, the cabs here are nothing like the ones back East. I apologize for the bumpy ride."

A grin split Louisa's face. "My father made carriages in Roxbury. You're right, these are not as elegant, but this is a new city with lots of growing to do. It will catch up."

"Did he now? I might have ridden in some of his carriages back there. What is his name?"

"Henry Hovey, but he left Boston in 1850 when the street cars cut into the need for carriages so severely. He moved to St. Louis and kept up the trade until he died."

"I'm sorry to hear that," the cabby nodded. "But your father sounds like a fine man if he made good carriages. And they are so much more enjoyable to ride in than being squashed in a noisy street car!"

"He would have been delighted to hear you say that. And yes, he was a good man."

"This town is growing so fast they already have horse-drawn cars going to the city's edges. Won't be long before I lose my place to them if some folks have their way."

"What is going on up ahead?" Louisa craned her neck to see a crowd outside an office building patiently waiting their turn to enter. "What do they sell there that has people so interested?"

"They don't sell anything," the cabby chuckled. "That's a land office. People go there to record the land plots they've already bought. In some places, people buy and sell horses or dry goods. Around here, it's all about land. Everybody is trying to guess where the city will expand next and wants to get ahead of it. Then, they can sell what they've bought at a profit. If I had some ready money, that's what I'd do," he mused.

Men shook hands as they met outside the office and doffed their hats to ladies who seemed intent on the same activity. That surprised Louisa. The women were there to record purchases, as they came with hands full of documents and maps.

As they rolled past, one woman caught her eye. Her gown was of a deep shade of russet, and her bonnet sported small feathers around the crown. She was engaged in animated discussion with a pair of men also waiting their turn and did not seem intimidated by them in the least. Louisa lost sight of the woman as they continued down the street, but she felt she would have liked to know her.

"Land trades hands around here so fast it's hard to keep up with it," the cabby said. This land here," he gestured to his right, "was all bought by Henry Brown. Now he's calling it the Brown Addition, thinking there will be homes all over it in the future. It's a gamble, though."

"Why? It looks like nice land."

"He gave ten acres in the middle of it to the Territory before Colorado was a state so they could build the state capitol on it. Then he started building a big house for himself over there."

She admired the multi-story home and realized that land had enabled Mr. Brown to turn his original money into a fortune.

"When will they build the Capitol?" she asked.

"Not fast enough for Brown, that's for sure. He's asking for his land back because they have not started building after fifteen years! The rumor is that they're still debating where to have the Capitol—here or in Golden."

"So Mr. Brown's gamble might not pay off."

"Oh, for now, it is. Brown has sold much of his land to speculators and just plain people who want to build a house in an area where the city hasn't stampeded over yet."

"So regular people are buying and selling land too? Not just rich people?" They rolled past farmland over a rise that gave a view of the city to the west.

"Like I said, if I had a few dollars, I'd be doing it, too. Now right over there," he pointed to the east, "is the ten acres Brown gave to the Territory for the Capitol. They call that Capitol Hill, even though nothing has been done with it. Suppose it would be a nice place to put it if they ever started to get serious."

The cab rolled on as the cabby pointed out points of interest and told her stories of his time in Denver. The two hours elapsed faster than she thought possible, but she had not had enough.

"Is there somewhere we could stop for a bite to eat? I'll buy your lunch if you'll keep driving me around."

A flash of teeth and a nod told her she had a deal. A few minutes later, they pulled up at an outdoor dining area where workmen from around the area were gathered. Some opened lunch pails, some purchased meals inside a small cafe, and some returned to the open air to eat. Louisa got out of the cab and bought large sandwiches, cups of coffee, and pieces of homemade pie. Dining under the sun felt like a picnic.

"I don't know your name," Louisa said around bites of her meal.

"Ralph," the cabby said, saluting her with his coffee cup. "And I thank you kindly for this lunch."

"I am Louisa. And I appreciate the touch of home in your voice and all the wonderful things you have shared with me today so far. Today has been just what I hoped I would experience."

They finished their meal, watered the horse, gave him Louisa's apple, and remounted the carriage. As the afternoon moved on, Ralph gave Louisa a bit of history about Denver: the gold rush, the coming of the trains, and the fire that destroyed a large section of the city and resulted in the red brick building materials she saw everywhere. It was a lazy ride, but it was full of interest to her.

"Stop!" Louisa cried suddenly. "Oh, stop!"

Ralph pulled up the reins, alarmed that something was amiss. Instead, he saw Louisa gazing across a field, shading her eyes to better see a figure standing amid the tall grass. It was a woman in a russet dress with a feathered hat. Louisa drew a deep breath.

"I want to meet that woman," she said, moving to the side of the cab. Ralph jumped down, assisted her, and moved as if to cross the field with her. "No, you stay with the horse. I'll be fine. I want to have a few words with her." He shook his head and pulled out his pipe.

Louisa lifted her skirts to wade through the grass but saw it was in vain; she would probably spend a good part of the evening removing burs from her hem. She shrugged and hurried on. The woman turned as she approached, shading her eyes.

"Hello! I am so sorry to bother you, but I wanted to meet you," Louisa said breathlessly. "I saw you outside the land office earlier today—at least that's what my cabby told me it was."

"Yes, I was there." The woman held out her ungloved hand. "My name is Melissa Hotchkiss. And you are...?"

"Louisa Hovey."

They shook hands, and Melissa's grip was firm and businesslike. Louisa gazed out across the land.

"Do you own this? It's lovely."

"I may own it in the future, but I haven't decided yet. I wanted to look at it myself before committing to it." The breeze ruffled the delicate feathers in Melissa's hat, and she put up a hand to ensure it did not blow off.

"I am just visiting Denver. But I am intrigued by all the land activity my cabby has told me about. What are you looking at to help you decide whether to buy this or not? How much of it will you buy?"

Melissa studied Louisa for a moment and seemed to make some judgment about her. She nodded and then turned to examine the field again. "It's not just the land. It's where the land is. And who owns it. Those are all as important as the ground itself."

Louisa made encouraging sounds.

"In this case, this is part of the Brown Addition..." she looked questioningly at Louisa, who nodded vigorously to indicate she understood the reference. "I have bought several pieces from Mr. Brown through intermediaries and have not regretted it. I've resold some at a profit. I am confident this will be a very important part of Denver someday. And I want to own some of it."

"So you don't care if it has a river nearby or trees or is rocky?"

"Well, rocky would be bad for building. New owners would undoubtedly cut down trees. A river can make it boggy. This particular area seems well-suited to home building. And now that I've seen it, I will ask Mr. Brown about it. Before the price goes up again," she laughed.

Louisa was enchanted. She looked at the field with new eyes that danced with excitement. "I don't mean to be rude, and you can tell me to mind my own business, but what would you pay for this? How much of it would you buy?"

Melissa nodded at the astute question. "Brown is selling plots right now that are about 50 feet wide and 125 feet deep, and he's asking $75." It's a steep price, but if the Capitol goes into this area, it will be a fraction of the land's value. I just sold some land for more than I paid and would like to buy four or five lots here. Are you interested in land, Louisa?"

"To be honest with you, I never thought of it in my life before today." She spun to take in the vista and faced the glorious mountains to the west. "I came here to see the West for myself. I'm a schoolteacher in Boston, and I'm visiting for a few weeks this summer. But I am captured by this place. I've only been here a day, and I already dread leaving to return back to the East."

21

Melissa rested a hand on Louisa's arm and said softly, "Somehow, when we met, I sensed you were the right kind of person to add to Denver. You may go back home, but I am sure you will return. Perhaps anchoring your heart here with a small piece of land is all you need to bring it about."

Louisa brought her hand to her chest and felt her pulse racing. *What an amazing thought!*

"You shouldn't buy land without thought," Melissa said, taking her arm and leading Louisa back across the field to her cab. "Where are you staying while you are in Denver? Perhaps we could meet."

"I am at the Windsor Hotel."

"A fine place. I have dined there often. Why don't we get together for dinner one day this week? Would Tuesday suit you?"

"I would enjoy that more than I can say," Louisa squeezed her new friend's hand. "Come at seven. I will meet you in the lobby."

The two women parted company as Louisa climbed back into the cab. Ralph tipped his hat to Melissa and asked if she wanted to ride back into town with them.

"I'm fine," she said, pointing to a delicate carriage and horse hidden under a stand of trees at the edge of the field. "Thank you for your consideration, though. I will see you on Tuesday, Louisa."

Louisa already knew that Tuesday was at least a century too long away.

CHAPTER 5

July 1881, Denver

Ralph and Louisa fell into an easy rhythm over the next four days, with the cab arriving at the Ladies' Entrance at ten each morning. Louisa put herself completely in his hands to show her everything in Denver. They roamed all the nooks and crannies of the city, explored the growing neighborhoods, ventured to the plains east of the city, and shared lunch each day at some small stand along the way.

Louisa went to church on Sunday, but Ralph drove her in the afternoon. She suddenly had a flash of guilt.

"Are you married, Ralph?"

The cabby smiled and nodded. "Yes. My Priscilla is the prettiest gal east or west of the Mississippi! We'd only been married a few months when I got the gold fever and moved us out here. She's a trooper."

"Oh, Ralph! Why didn't you say so? Here, I've been monopolizing your time for days!"

Ralph chuckled. "Honestly, I've enjoyed our travels through the city, and if I wasn't escorting you, I would be wandering the streets looking for other fares." A red blush crawled up his neck. "And the money doesn't go amiss either."

Somewhat mollified, Louisa raised the idea that had been brewing in her for a few days. "I would like to go right up into the mountains, Ralph, right up to them. I'm sure it would take all day long to go and come back. What if you bring Priscilla and we make an adventure of it?"

Ralph hesitated. "Well, our little girl. . ."

"You have children? How wonderful!"

"Just my girl, Betsy. She's six. I'm sure Priscilla could find another woman to take care of her for the day," he mused.

"Nonsense! Bring her along. It will be fun! I'll get the hotel to make up a picnic lunch, and we'll set off early. What do you think?" Louisa leaned forward in her seat, trying to see his face better. She vibrated with excitement.

"Now wouldn't that be a treat!" Ralph cried. "Betsy has never been to the mountains. Neither has Priscilla now that I think of it. And I know just the place to go where you can see them best."

"Then it's settled. We'll do it tomorrow." Louisa sank back into the seat and began to plan what she would wear and what to ask for in the picnic basket.

"Thank you, Miss Louisa," Ralph ducked his head. "It would be our pleasure to go with you."

"No 'Miss' Louisa now Ralph. We've been batting around town all week together. Let's continue as friends, all right?"

The cabby nodded. Then, knowing the day was coming to an end and that she was interested in the area, he drove slowly past the acreage where she'd met Melissa Hotchkiss. He was not wrong.

Louisa leaned out of the carriage as they went past.

~ ~ ~

Monday broke clear and sunny, much to Louisa's satisfaction. Ralph, Priscilla, and little Betsy arrived at eight in the morning, just after Louisa had finished a hearty breakfast and gathered her day things from her room. Betsy was bouncing on the seat in eagerness, her light brown pigtails whipping like twin pinwheels.

Priscilla wore a light blue cotton dress that Louisa was sure was her "Sunday best" and had added a small black hat. She was shy in Louisa's presence until Betsy's incessant chatter broke the ice. She pointed to a cloud and declared it a horse, then crowed with delight when a cat jumped in the air after a butterfly, and gazed in wonder at Louisa's flowery hat.

"Would you sit on my lap?" Louisa asked softly, admiring the girl's energy and intelligence. Without hesitation, Betsy climbed up and nestled in the grey silk of Louisa's ample bosom. As she played with the ribbons of Louisa's hat, she wormed her way into the older woman's heart, and Priscilla became more friendly.

"Thank you for inviting us. It's been so long since Ralph had a day to spend on an excursion like this," she said. "He has been talking about you all week and all the interesting places you've been going."

"The pleasure has been mine, I assure you. I'm far from home, and having someone like Ralph show me the city has been perfect. I am in love with Denver. You are so lucky to live here!"

Ralph guffawed quietly. "As if she had any choice," he murmured. Priscilla slapped him playfully on the arm, and Louisa smiled.

"I have been longing to go to the mountains since I first glimpsed them from the train." Louisa's eyes fastened on the vista ahead of them as they traveled across Denver. The horse moved steadily and seemed to know where it was going and what a climb it would be. "I teach school back in Boston," she told Betsy, "but my students are all little boys who drive me crazy, not sweet girls like you." Betsy smiled, and Louisa caught the mischief hidden behind the pretty facade. She sensed the girl was as much a handful as her most rambunctious student back home.

"I came west this summer because I have been teaching about this country for years but have never seen it." She turned seriously to Betsy. When you grow up, my dear, never be afraid to go see what you want to see, just like your parents have done by moving here. Life is boring without adventures." The child nodded solemnly.

With a sigh of contentment, Louisa fixed her eyes on the mountains once more, and the closer they drew to them, the less she spoke. The landscape's sheer beauty and the soaring wall's rugged mass left her speechless. Betsy played with a doll she had brought along or bounced from her mother's lap to the seat next to her father and back again. Priscilla breathed in the fresh air and turned her pale face to the sun.

Hours later, true to his word, Ralph turned the horse off the path in a perfect picnic spot and got down from the cab to help the women. Betsy required no assistance, having already hopped down and run off after a clacking grasshopper. Great swaths of aspen trees, gleaming white in the brightness of the day, ringed the meadow. Their trembling leaves and the soughing of the wind through nearby pines were music to Louisa's ears.

"Oh, how lovely!" Louisa clapped her hands together and clutched them to her chest. Her lungs strained at the thin air, and her eyes were alight with delightful sparkle. She turned slowly in one direction and then another, gazing at the beauty around her. She hardly noticed when Betsy placed a tiny bouquet of orange and blue wildflowers in her hand.

Priscilla busied herself, spreading a blanket on the ground and opening the large picnic basket. She gasped when she saw the contents. A whole chicken, sandwiches of creamed cheese and cucumber, fruit tarts and cookies, and an assortment of other small containers of interesting side dishes greeted her eyes. The kitchen staff had nestled a bottle of wine for the adults and one of milk for Betsy in the corners of the basket. Cutlery and napkins completed the picture.

"Goodness, what a lot of food," she marveled. Tantalizing smells escaped the containers as she set them out, drawing even Betsy back from her explorations and breaking Louisa's mountain gazing spell. Ralph rubbed his hands together in anticipation as they all sat down to eat.

"When I first came out here I was intent on mining gold like I told you," Ralph said as he consumed bites of potato salad. "I came up here with a buddy to explore and came across this place. I probably sat here half the day just enjoying the view. We camped out that night right over there," he gestured to the side of the clearing, "and by the time we went back to Denver, I was pretty sure I loved the mountains but was not ready to break my back in them. That's when I took my grubstake and bought a horse and cab."

"Very smart of you," Louisa said. "I see a lot of rough men in town who have been up here mining and don't have much to show for it. But look at you—you have your wife, your daughter, steady employment, and a future ahead of you if you're careful with your money."

"He's planning to buy another cab soon and hire another driver," Priscilla said with quiet pride. Ralph sat up taller and took another sip of the light wine.

Louisa pushed the plate of chicken closer to Priscilla, and her keen eyes dropped for a moment to the woman's waistline. "Have some more, dear, and please take the leftovers home for your dinner tonight," she said. Priscilla's cheeks were a delightful pink, and her glance slid to Ralph. Louisa knew she'd guessed correctly that the family would add a member this year.

They spent a lazy afternoon wandering among the trees, lounging on the grass for brief naps, and watching Betsy have a long conversation with the horse as he ate carrots from her hand. When it was finally time to pack up the rest of the picnic, shake out the blanket, and step up into the cab again, Louisa knew this would be a memory to treasure for the rest of her life.

~   ~   ~

Dearest Harriet:

My education must have been faulty, for I find myself completely out of words to describe the day I have had today. Ralph and his family and I went up into the mountains themselves for a picnic, and I felt I had died and gone to heaven. There is such a weight to the mountains and a presence about them. There is no way to capture it in little squiggles on the page.

Tomorrow, I will have dinner with my new friend, Melissa Hotchkiss. She is coming to the hotel, and we will dine in the hall downstairs. We will have much to say to one another as we seem like kindred spirits. Not like you and me, of course, for we have been friends since we learned what the word meant for the first time. However, it is exciting to contemplate getting to know an adult that I believe will significantly change my life. Call it what you will, but I think life is about to turn a corner for me.

I'll stop for tonight and will pick this up after my dinner tomorrow. Sleep tight, Harriet. I know I will.

Fondly,
Louisa

Chapter 6

July 1881, Denver

"If I'd packed less clothing, I would not be wasting all this time!" Louisa groaned, gazing at her reflection in the long mirror. Her gown was pearl colored with accents of apricot at the throat, hemline, and sleeve cuffs. She knew she looked good in apricot. Now, she wondered if anything would make her look good.

After three changes of outfits, her curly hair defied its usual neat precision, and she was sweating. She sighed again. "This is just dinner with a new friend. Why am I fretting?" She dropped into a chair and fanned herself with her plump hand. Then she rose and began unbuttoning the dress, intent on putting the green one back on.

"That's enough, Louisa," she said when she had it settled on her sturdy frame. "Green it is. Green like grass. Green like... land." That brought a smile to her face at last, and she began to resettle her curls. Once her accessories were in place, she took another glance at the clock and hurried out of her room.

A delicious breeze blew through the lobby's open doors at the Ladies' Entrance. Louisa sank onto a settee that looked more comfortable than it was. Her eyes fastened on the doorway, and when Melissa swept through it, she rose quickly and waved to her.

"Hello! I'm so glad you've come," Louisa said. Melissa's broad smile was all the confirmation she needed that she had not imagined the warmth of friendship between them in the windswept field.

"I've been looking forward to it," the other woman said warmly. I've been so busy since last week that I could use an evening to talk and be still." Melissa slipped her arm through Louisa's, and together, they turned toward the light and noise of the hotel dining room.

Louisa was pleased that having a guest rated her a better table. The fact that the waitstaff knew Melissa by name helped, too. "Mrs. Hotchkiss. So nice to see you again," the *maitre d'hotel* bowed slightly. He gestured to one of his staff and murmured, "Table Six." His assistant whisked them across the room to an area Louisa had only gazed upon previously. He pulled out chairs, and both women nodded their thanks as white linen napkins landed on their laps.

Perusing the menu took a few minutes, with decadent dishes arrayed across the page for their selection. Louisa chose the lamb, and Melissa picked a hearty beef pie. When the waiter took their orders and departed, both sat back and looked at each other.

Taking a sip of water, Louisa said, "Tell me about you. Tell me about your life here in Denver. Tell me everything."

"Oh, Louisa! That would take far too long." Melissa's laugh tinkled in the candlelit air. "I'll give you the short version." She slowly turned her water glass on the table as she spoke.

"I moved to Denver from San Francisco with my husband ten years ago. He died two years ago. He was the one who dreamed of coming here, but I fell in love with Colorado and decided to stay. I cast about for a way to make a living and stumbled upon an opportunity to work for someone building homes in different parts of the city. After a year, I realized that my real passion was the land itself, not the building process. So I sold some land my uncle left me, took my assets, and bought what I could. Fortune favors the innocent, they say, and I was blessed to be able to resell my first piece of land for several times what I paid for it. The real estate bug bit me then, and I have continued to repeat the process ever since."

Melissa's story carried Louisa. She smiled in delight at the ideas it raised. "And the other day, you were buying more land. On speculation—isn't that what they call it? Not for yourself but to sell later?"

"Absolutely. I have a piece of property that is my own, and I keep it for sentimental reasons. I will build on it in a year or two. But I am quite happy in a boarding house and spending my days exploring the next land boom area."

With a sigh, Louisa sat back and shook her head in admiration. "I can just hear what my family in Boston would say about living the way you do." She chuckled. "They would be astonished. Appalled actually. But it is so exciting to me."

Melissa leaned forward across the table. "You could do it too, Louisa. I know you could. You have the interest and the beginnings of a love for this area. What's to stop you?"

Now Louisa laughed in earnest. "What, indeed? Except for the small issue of money and family approval."

"Money, bah!" Melissa snorted. "You can always get money somewhere. But is your family's approval so important to you? I sense you came out here this summer without much enthusiasm from them. Am I right?"

heir meals arrived, and Louisa took her first few delicious bites while considering Melissa's comments. At last, she set her fork down and sipped light wine.

"As for the second question, they didn't want me to come. My sister-in-law and my best friend were encouraging, but the rest of the family is probably still in shock. Yet here I am. So I guess it's not a primary concern to me now that I've broken the mold, so to speak." She gazed unseeing around the elegant room. "But money, well, that's harder to give up than family approval. I do have a little that my father left me when he died. As my brother says, that's for my old age."

31

Melissa shook her head vigorously. "And who says you will live to be old? You have to live now, Louisa. Today. You can build your life to be whatever you want it to be. But you have to take some risks. When I bought my first property, my heart was in my mouth. I pictured going broke and losing everything, ending up on the street or—far worse—having to crawl back to my family in San Francisco." She shuddered.

"I decided the risk was worth the possible loss and went forward. After I got over that first purchase, I have never looked back. And I never will. You can make money here and live as you wish, but you must be bold enough to grab it."

Her heart beating like a caged bird in her chest, Louisa took another sip of wine to calm herself—and then another for good measure. Melissa waited her out.

"I wouldn't have the first idea how to get started," she said quietly. "I'm not as brave as you."

"I'm not brave," Melissa said. "I'm just willing to step forward until I fall into a hole. And if I do, then I'll climb out and keep going. That's what real people do, Louisa. Do you want to be an old maid schoolteacher in Boston until you die living on the memories of a wonderful summer in Denver, regretting that you never grabbed life by the tail? Or do you want to live right now?"

Both women remained silent as they finished their entrees. When fruit, cheese, and cakes arrived with coffee, they were still lost in their thoughts. At last, Louisa focused on her companion again and said, "Let's take a walk on the terrace, shall we?"

They rose and left the dining room, drawn by the cool evening outside after the filling meal. Even in the darkness, the presence of the mountains to the west, with the dying sunset silhouetting their peaks, caused Louisa to lean over the railing in wonder. "I want to put down roots here," she said softly. "I want to say I live in Denver. I want to shed my lifelong hesitancy and become a bolder person." She turned to Melissa.

"Will you teach me?"

Melissa gave her a gentle hug and nodded. "Tomorrow, we'll explore and find a place you can call your own. And then we'll find another place you can use as the beginnings of your new life, your new empire." Both of them laughed as the tension of the evening dissipated.

~   ~   ~

Dearest Harriet,

I'm about to do something crazy--more than coming West, more than anything I've ever done. And I can't wait to tell you all about it. But for tonight, my friend, let me say that the person who returns to Boston in two weeks will not be the same one who left.

I won't spoil the secret. You'll have to wait until I can write more. I will seal this letter once I've begun my metamorphosis. Sorry to tease you, but at least all you have to do is turn the page to learn more.

Affectionately,
Louisa

~   ~   ~

Louisa bit her lip nervously as she rode in Melissa's carriage the next morning. The day was fresh, with white clouds dotting the sky and birds singing in the meadows they passed. Still, her anxiety over the step she was contemplating kept her from enjoying it all.

"Those frown lines will become permanent if you don't let them go right now," Melissa said, patting her friend's arm. "We're just going out to look at beautiful land. What's to worry about?"

A small smile crept across Louisa's face as she relaxed her corrugated forehead. "It's easy for you. You've done this many times. I'm just worried I'll make a mistake and regret it later."

"That's why we're doing this together. I made all the mistakes you can make, and I won't let you repeat them. People have talked

33

me into worthless land. I've passed by great pieces of property and assumed they were not ready for development yet. I've sat on my money out of fear of the future. I've been swindled, sidestepped, underestimated, and talked down to for being a woman doing business." Melissa smiled as she gently drew her horse to the verge of the road and guided it under a tree. "And I still keep coming back. I've made mistakes, but they haven't killed me. If anything, it's made me smarter."

Louisa looked at Melissa in admiration and shook her head. "I like you more and more, Melissa."

With a satisfied nod, Melissa tied the reins and began to get down from the carriage. When they were both on the ground, she took a moment to give her horse a few carrots and a fond pat on the neck. Then, they turned to survey the area around them.

"I suppose you've heard the rumors about the Capitol, haven't you?"

"Just a little," Louisa shook her head.

"Henry Brown gave his ten acres right over there," Melissa shaded her eyes and pointed to the south, "and they've done nothing with them so far. There's great debate about whether the Capitol should be here or in Golden. Mr. Brown has made a lot of money selling land around this so-called Capitol Hill in anticipation of the seat of government going there. Now it's all just dangling in the balance of some politicians trying to make up their minds."

"Do you think it will be here? What is Golden like?"

"Oh, it will be in Denver, trust me. Golden has less energy and commerce than Denver. Speculators are using the uncertainty to sell land in Golden by saying the state may build the Capitol there. But I've staked my fortune on it being here, and I think I'm right."

"And if you're not right?"

"I stand to lose a lot of money. . . but I'll still have the land. You see, Louisa, buying land is never stupid. I might make less reselling it than I would if there were activity on Capitol Hill by now, but it's still land. It's permanent. Solid. Always worth something."

As she studied the fields around them, Louisa strolled out from under the shade of the trees to get a better view. Melissa followed her. They walked in one direction, then another, as Louisa considered what her friend and mentor had said. The pull of the land on her was fierce. If it just wasn't for the money!

Finally, Melissa broke the silence. "What holds you back, Louisa?"

"I'll be honest. I'm afraid to spend the little money I have on speculation." She shook her head. "In some ways, my brother Charles is right. I need to think of the future and protect what I have."

"And I told you we can find money. Don't think of it as a finite bowl of something precious. Instead, view it as a fountain. Water comes in, rises in the air, sparkles, then falls and circles again. Money is like that. You have to spend it—send it into the air—to make it shine and bring delight. There's always more if you know where to look."

Melissa faced Louisa and put a hand on her arm. "I'll be blunt. How much do you have to invest?"

Louisa was usually hesitant to discuss money, but she felt trust rise in her. "I have $500. That still leaves me with some to make me feel secure, but it is all I can spare. I can't afford to lose it either."

"Fine. That's just perfect. Get back in the carriage."

"Where are we going?" Louisa lagged behind Melissa as the other woman strode across the grassy field.

"We're going to look at your first land."

Louisa gulped, but moved toward the carriage.

~   ~   ~

Two men and two horses stood at the edge of the land Melissa drove them to. One man gestured, and the other shook his head. The gesturing became more intense, and so did the shaking of the head. At last, the skeptical man waved off the other man and got on his horse. He rode away without a backward glance.

"Pick some wildflowers," Melissa instructed a surprised Louisa. "Just do it."

Louisa bent and gathered a handful of bright orange columnar Indian Paintbrushes and shooting star-shaped Columbine. The combination pleased her, but she was confused about the purpose of what they were doing. Out of the corner of her eye, she watched Melissa covertly watch the man. He, in turn, looked out over the land, checked his pocket watch, and glanced at them.

"A lovely day," Melissa called with her hand on her bonnet and a sunny smile. "This is a beautiful place." The man tipped his hat and strolled in their direction.

"You ladies are welcome to gather all the flowers you like," he said, nodding at their handfuls of blooms. "This is my land, but nobody will say I'm stingy with the plants."

Melissa laughed. "Why, thank you, sir. We would have asked first if I had known it was your land. It's just such a rare day we couldn't resist."

Louisa tried to keep the puzzlement off her face. *What on earth is Melissa doing?* It felt like she was watching a play on an outdoor stage.

"I hoped you might have to ask that other fellow since I was trying to sell this to him, but he's not interested. Another one who thinks the Golden rumors are true, I guess." The man shook his head and took a handkerchief from his pocket to wipe his brow, looking after the receding horse and rider.

"Oh, just think of owing some of this land!" Melissa gushed, turning to Louisa. "Wouldn't that be grand, Louisa?" Taking her cue, Louisa nodded an looked to the west to admire the mountains.

"Think of having this view for the rest of your life," she said, using Melissa's same light tone.

Melissa watched the man and asked almost breathlessly, "How much are you selling it for? I might know someone who would like it."

The man perked up. "This piece is ten lots. Each one is fifty feet wide and more than twice that deep. I'm asking a hundred dollars for each lot. You can tell your friends that."

Melissa made a shocked O of her mouth. "My, that's a lot of money!" She paused and frowned. "You know, I heard some people are selling lots like this for sixty dollars each. Why are yours so high?"

The man's gaze sharpened. "If they are, they are underselling. That's ridiculous. This land will be worth a lot when they get around to building the Capitol over there," he pointed. Shading her eyes, Melissa looked south and shook her head. "Doesn't look like they're doing anything at all," she said. "Not at all."

"I'm sure they will. Really." The man warmed to his topic. "I gave the Territory the land. They said they'd build there. I know it's just a matter of time."

Melissa turned back to him. "But Golden. . . ?"

He snorted. "Rumors and poppycock. Don't pay any attention."

"Still, don't you think buying would be a great risk until they settle that question?"

"And when it's settled, the land will be selling for two hundred or more for each lot," he asserted.

Melissa bent and plucked another daisy to add to her bouquet. "I wonder if you'd consider seventy-five dollars for a lot? It would be so nice to own something like this."

The man took off his hat and scratched his head. "If you're serious, we can shake on that price right now. Seventy-five for a lot."

Something glimmered in Melissa's eyes. She put out her hand, and they shook as she said, "That's perfect. We'll take all ten lots."

Louisa squeaked.

Too late, the man saw that this innocent-looking woman had carefully led him down the path. He stared at her, his hand still gripping hers, trying to work out what had just happened.

"Who are you?" he whispered.

The grin that broke across Melissa's face was radiant. "I'm Melissa Hotchkiss, Mr. Brown. And I am happy to meet you face-to-face at last. Shall we make an appointment to meet at the land office tomorrow morning and sign the deeds?"

Mr. Brown stumbled back a small step. "Miss Hotchkiss! You've been buying land all over town!" He shook his head in admiration. "I admit you took me in." He glanced at Louisa, who was a witness to the agreement. "And I'll stand by our bargain. Lesson learned."

Louisa joined Melissa in her laughter and tried to quiet the rising panic bubble in her chest. They'd just bought ten lots! She didn't have the money for that! What was Melissa playing at?

They set a time to conclude their business at the land office in the morning. Melissa and Louisa returned in their carriage as Mr. Brown gave a somewhat sheepish wave and rode off on his horse.

"And that's the way you do it," Melissa said, looking Louisa in the eyes. "Never let them see you coming, and be sure to leave them admiring your ability in bargaining."

"But you bought ten lots! That's $750. I only have five hundred."

"No, you now have $125 left to get another piece of land or to hold onto for living expenses when you move out here to Denver. Five of the lots will be mine; five will be yours. You pick which five. Together, we've just scooped wily Henry Brown, and we're going to make a killing when that Capitol goes up. You watch."

With a snap of the reins, a satisfied Melissa guided the horse back onto the road, and Louisa felt a tide of anticipation lift her almost out of her seat. I own five lots of land in Denver!

Chapter 7

July 1881, traveling

Louisa had already worn the paper slightly by handling it repeatedly. She found her mind and heart anchored where she'd been, not where she was headed as the country scenery rolled past her train carriage window. It felt like a dream, but she had the paper.

> Grantor: Henry Cordes Brown, Denver, Colorado
> Grantee: Louisa Jane Hovey, Boston, Massachusetts
> Five lots of Brown's Addition, to whit…

She fixated on the first two lines above the dense legal description of the exact placement of the lots. Grantor, grantee. *That was her!*

Melissa had graciously let her choose which of the ten lots she wanted for herself and then took title to the remaining five. Louisa chose those that were westernmost with a view of the mountains. Melissa was indifferent to the view but was delighted with the purchase. Their time at the land office showed Louisa how active the land market was. They waited patiently in line and then stepped up to the clerk. After paying a small fee, Louisa watched the clerk's pen fill in those wonderful lines in the book with beautiful handwriting: *Grantor; Grantee. Louisa Jane Hovey.*

She reverently took her copy of the deed from the clerk and looked at Melissa with shining eyes. Mr. Brown shook hands with both of them, and she knew he'd be more careful around women regarding land from that point forward. She suppressed a smile, but Melissa squeezed her arm and grinned at her.

When they stepped back out of the office into the brisk breeze, the sun glinted on everything that touched Louisa's eyes. The air seemed even thinner than usual, if possible, as she had trouble catching her breath.

"Now you belong to Denver, and part of it belongs to you," Melissa whispered.

A week later, she was speeding back to Boston, back to sure consternation from her family, back to significant decisions and activity on her part and great interference on theirs. But she had her paper, and her path was clear.

She slipped the document back into her traveling bag and looked at the increasingly congested landscape. Cheyenne, Chicago, Pittsburgh, and Albany had all passed without her attention. She changed trains when necessary, oversaw her luggage, and was now on the final leg of her journey. But she wasn't going home.

The paper in her bag meant Boston would never be "home" again. Her family, her friends, and the children in her class lived there, but for her, there was nowhere but Denver anymore. She resisted the impulse to pull out the paper again. It was too precious to risk now that people were beginning to gather belongings and jostle one another in preparation for arrival at the Boston station.

Louisa let others leave the train first, knowing hurrying was pointless. She would only stand waiting on the platform for her trunk to appear, so she might as well sit comfortably. When her turn came to step down from the train, Louisa was surprised to see

Harriet and Louise-Caroline hurrying toward her. They embraced her, hugged her tight, and exclaimed how wonderful she looked.

"How did you know I'd arrive today?" Louisa said, pleased they'd made an effort to be there.

"We've been meeting trains for two days. We couldn't wait to hear all about your adventures!" Harriet hopped from one tiny foot to the other in excitement. The waiting had not dimmed her keenness or her smile.

"Welcome home, Louisa!" Louise-Caroline gave her another hug. "It's been so dull here for the weeks while you were away. Harriet has shared all your letters with me except the last one. She has kept that one a secret, and now I want to know what is going on."

"Let's go have some tea. I'm famished," Louisa pointed toward the station restaurant. As they began to move away from the platform, Harriet gave a porter instructions about Louisa's trunk and then caught up to them at the dining room door. A waiter quickly seated them, and they sank to their seats, examining each other for changes in their time apart.

"I have so much to tell you," Louisa said. "But first, is there any news I need to know from here? I don't want you to burst at the seams to tell me something while I'm rattling on about my trip."

Her sister-in-law smiled. "Nothing noteworthy. I managed to talk Charles down from the ceiling after you left, but I think he's getting close to there again as he anticipates giving you a good talking-to."

Louisa rolled her eyes and sighed. "What is it with men, especially older brothers and fathers, that they just can't get it through their heads that the women around them have their own ideas? Goodness. I didn't miss that while I was away."

Harriet could stand it no longer. "Louisa, tell her. Tell her what you did. I knew you wanted it to come from you, so I didn't show her the last part of your last letter. Which, I must say, was a week ago, and so I am also not up to date on your doings."

With a small smile, Louisa turned to Louise-Caroline. "I thank you again for your gift before I left. I did what you told me to do and used it to buy a souvenir. Do you want to see it?"

Louise-Caroline nodded eagerly. "Yes! What did you bring back?"

Louisa reached into her bag, pulled out the paper, and laid it before her sister-in-law. Harriet craned her neck to get a look at it as well. Louise-Caroline frowned.

"What am I looking at?"

"Read it." Louisa sat back to watch her. As realization dawned on Louise-Caroline's beautiful face, Louisa was grateful that Harriet had withheld the news. It was enjoyable to see her surprise and awe.

"Oh, Louisa! Is this a deed? You bought *land??*"

Louisa folded her hands, resting her elbows on the chair arms, and nodded.

"What a surprise!" Louise-Caroline shook her head. She looked from the paper to Louisa again. "But what are you going to do with it?" Her bewilderment was just a foretaste of the storm Louisa could anticipate from the rest of the family.

"I plan to sell it." The other women stared at her. "At a profit." Their eyes opened wider. "And then I will buy some more."

~　　~　　~

Dear Louisa,

I trust you have arrived in Boston safe and sound and are settling back into your daily routine. But don't settle too much. You know where you belong, and I can't wait until you return.

I've already had interested buyers on some of our ten purchased lots. People are just land-crazy here right now. The middle lots have the most activity for now—two of yours, three of mine. Let's sell them as a block. We will make a substantial profit since *bundling them together means we can ask for $800. We will each more than double our investments.*

You said you trusted me to handle the land transactions until you return. I appreciate your confidence in me. I will cable you when these lots sell. The money you make will begin to build a nest egg for you for the future. I'll also keep my eye out for suitable parcels.

I know you are partial to the two lots to the west; this potential sale does not include them. You'll still have them but don't get sentimentally attached. It will get in your way when it comes time to profit from them.

Your friend,
Melissa Hotchkiss

~ ~ ~

When Louisa returned from her trip, the avalanche of advice and condemnation she had anticipated was nothing compared to reality. She seriously worried her half-brother Charles would get their sister Rebecca to lock her in her room. Fortunately, she was of an age that the law was on her side, as was Charles' wife, Louise-Caroline.

Sunday dinners became tense affairs. Charles glowered. Rebecca's mother-in-law tut-tutted. Rebecca and George did their best to soothe ruffled feathers and invited extra guests to keep the meal from degenerating into a shouting match. Even Charles, a well-bred gentleman and an officer, could not break etiquette far enough to censor her in front of near strangers.

Louisa floated above the fray and fixed her eyes on her plans. Each day, she rose and said to herself, "A year from now, I'll be getting out of bed in Denver!" Each Sunday dinner was one less to endure, though she knew the tension would only grow as her relocation drew nearer. But her piece of paper and Melissa's cheery letters sustained her. Already, the paper was out of date. Two of her lots sold. Melissa held new documents for her, including some fresh purchases.

It was enough to make her giddy sometimes. She was still sitting in the parlor in Boston, and yet her initial investment was growing. She'd have kicked herself if she had not bought the first five lots, but how hard it was to lay down the funds the first time. Now, with Melissa's help, she was becoming used to it.

As her students filed into the classroom to start the school year and took their seats, banging books and other items around as only boys do, she smiled at them in a new way. She was going to miss a few of them. Guy Holliday, in particular. What funny creatures boys were—especially when she knew she would not have to endure them much longer.

"I have an announcement today," she began after they settled somewhat. Her radiant expression caught their attention. "This will be the last year I will be teaching you." Gasps met her words, and whispering began.

"Why?" Henry exclaimed. "Did we do something wrong?"

Louisa laughed; they'd never seen her do so before. They stared. "Oh, Henry, it is all your fault. It isn't what you did wrong, though. It's what you did right. You challenged me. You asked me what was good about the West. And so I went to see for myself this past summer. It is a good territory that is wide open for growth. I've bought land there and want to be part of that growth."

A half dozen conversations broke out as the boys shook their heads and tried to make sense of their teacher's plans. She dusted the ubiquitous chalk from her fingers and clapped to get their attention again.

"Let me show you what it's like." She began to pass out penny postcards to each boy with images of Denver, the West, the Rocky Mountains, the Transcontinental Railroad, real Indians, mountain men, and more. She'd brought home enough for every boy to have one, and they all gathered around to pass them among themselves. Their eyes devoured the pictures.

"The most important lesson I can teach you, boys, is to question what other people tell you. Explore the world for yourself. Your schoolbooks have good information. But personal experience is better. The West was bigger, broader, wilder, and more beautiful than I could imagine. I've put a stake in the ground there and plan to return next year.

"That was my dream." She fixed them with a glowing gaze. "What's yours?"

CHAPTER 8

Boston, 1881

"I understand you are a school teacher, Miss Hovey," the distinguished man to Louisa's left leaned toward her during the soup course one evening. "What made you choose to do that?"

Somewhat surprised, Louisa took stock of her questioner. He was handsome enough with greying hair and a drooping mustache. She was pleased to see that he knew how to eat soup without any of it lingering on the hair over his lip. She gave a half smile and nodded to him.

"I teach young boys at the Lewis School," she said, taking a small sip of her wine as she gauged his interest. He nodded and looked like he wanted to hear more. "My class is full of energetic youngsters who will one day go on to do great things. Not because I am teaching them you understand, but because of the day in which we live. Our country is on the brink of a mighty explosion of growth and opportunity."

The candles glinted in the man's eyes. He tipped his head slightly and appeared thoughtful. "I think I know what you mean," he said.

"There is something in the air, isn't there?"

"Oh yes, most certainly. When I was in Denver last summer, the streets fairly pulsed with it!" She was about to say more when a cough from her brother Charles' end of the table drew her up short.

Swallowing the eagerness she had been about to impart, she judiciously took another sip of wine instead.

It irked her, to say the least, to have to govern her words so closely. She longed to tell this kind man about what she'd seen and experienced in the West and her imminent plans. But both Charles and her half-sister Rebecca's husband George forbade it. Because she lived under George's roof, she obeyed—for now.

When she announced her plans to move permanently to Denver a few months after returning from her trip, the explosion in the parlor during after-dinner coffee nearly toppled her from her chair.

"Oh, Louisa! Not this nonsense again!" Charles had barked. "I permitted you, with great reluctance, to take a trip to Denver this past summer. But this idea of actually moving there—I won't bear it."

"You can't mean it," George began. "You're just swept up in what you experienced out there. Just let it cool down, and you'll see sense again." Ever the conciliator, George did his best to pour oil on the choppy family waves she'd stirred.

"Aren't you happy here with us?" Rebecca's coffee cup rattled in its thin china saucer. "Is there more we could do to make this house more comfortable for you?"

A muttered, "Spoiled woman losing her mind," came from George's mother's corner of the room where she worked on a particularly elaborate piece of tatting. "I warned George about this family. . .."

The news was not new to Louise-Caroline, and she busied herself with her spoon, stirring cream into her coffee and looking over the plate of petite fours. For good measure, she let out a small gasp. It would never do for Charles to think she was in on the plan. But she also managed a tiny wink in her sister-in-law's direction.

"It's not nonsense," Louisa said, setting her cup and saucer squarely on the serving table. "And I don't recall you *permitting* me to go to Denver either. You didn't speak to me for weeks before or after the trip. Do I have to remind you that I am a 41-year-old woman? You may be my older half-brother but not my keeper."

Charles huffed into his enormous mustache and sputtered. When he prepared to launch into speech again, she cut him off.

Louisa addressed the three she lived with and toned down her voice.

"I am most grateful for the home you have given me for these many years, my dears," she said. "I have enjoyed our peace as well as our times of laughter. I will miss you all and intend to come back to visit when it is feasible."

"Oh, how gracious of you, Lady Bountiful," Charles sneered. "And where will you find the money to do all this traveling? Don't look at me; that's all I can say!"

The others swiveled from Charles' stern face to Louisa's placid one, awaiting her response. The coffee went cold in their cups.

"Father left you the bulk of his estate as the eldest brother," Louisa said, "as was his right to do. But he left me a little, too. And while in Denver, I used some of that money to invest in land."

If Charles had looked surprised before, he was positively thunderstruck now. Red that had circled his tight collar now began to flood upward. His eyes flashed, and his cup and saucer clattered to the mantelpiece where he'd been standing. There was no cutting him off this time.

"You *what???* Of all the silly, stupid, idiotic things to do. You've lost the money I told you to set aside for your old age! We won't always be here to prop you up, Louisa. What are you going to do then? Eh?" He wiped his forehead with his palm. "I can't believe what I'm hearing." He turned his back to her. "The rest of you talk some sense back into her. I'm speechless."

Again, the other faces turned her way. Louisa still sat calmly. She eyed her brother's steely back and shook her head sadly. She'd hoped to gain his support but hadn't really expected it.

"I plan to travel on my own money, Charles," she said gently. "I not only bought land in Denver, but I have an agent there. Subsequently, I sold half of that land at a great profit. And then I bought more land. I intend to do the same with it. I have more than tripled the money I had when I started. I believe I will be fine."

Charles slowly rotated back toward her as she had spoken, his mouth agape. George's mother's ball of yarn dropped to the floor and rolled several feet unheeded. Rebecca almost sagged back against the back of the couch where she sat but caught herself and remained lady-straight as she stared at her sister. Louise-Caroline reached for another tiny cake and placed it on her plate.

Charles sank into a chair as his mouth opened and closed several times without words. Louisa straightened her skirts and rose. "I think that's enough discussion for one evening, don't you? I was only informing you of my plans. I will be leaving on June first."

Over subsequent days, there were many whispered conversations, manly discussions over glasses of port in the study after dinner between Charles and George, and general consternation in the household. Louisa waited it out. Nobody could do anything about her plans, so she could be calm.

Finally, her brother and brother-in-law sat with her to lay down the law.

"I am completely in disagreement with you, Louisa. I want you to know that in no uncertain terms." Charles stood and began to pace before her and George. "You are disrupting this whole family and will make yourself a laughing stock. That will rub off on all of us. Do you understand?"

"Why should what I do be of any interest to anyone else in Boston? I'm an aging unmarried school teacher. Nobody's paid me the least notice. I can't see that changing." Louisa worked to keep her voice level. It would do no good to fuel his rage.

"Well, they'll notice now! And your sister Rebecca will bear the brunt of it when visiting other ladies. George's mother will hear about it in church. George might well lose business because his family is proving unreliable."

Louisa chuckled. "I hardly think it will come to that. The only way people will know this is what I plan to do is if you go around the city telling them. I don't intend to, other than my closest friends. And for your information, they are excited and supportive."

"This is a disaster. George, tell her what is going to happen." Again, he turned his back to his sister.

George cleared his throat. "Charles and I have talked about this a great deal, Louisa. We've come to some... guidelines... we'd like you to follow if you insist on taking this course."

"I do intend it. What are these 'guidelines'?"

Unable to contain himself, Charles jumped back into the discussion. "We will hear no more about it. Do you understand? As long as you live here in Boston under George's roof, visit my home, and interact with people we know, you will not speak of your so-called plan. Period. What you think about and do in your room is up to you. But this is how it will be. I will not have this ludicrous idea of yours dogging my life and personal peace daily. That's it."

Louisa turned to George. "And you concur?"

George glanced at Charles and looked uncomfortable. He whispered, stopped, cleared his throat again, and started anew. "Yes. Yes, I see the sense in what Charles is saying. It's upsetting to think of you going so far away into the unknown where we can't protect you. And I know Rebecca will miss you terribly."

Touched, Louisa patted George's arm. "That's kind of you to say. I will miss you all too, as I have said. And because I respect you and want nothing but tranquility in your home, I will hold my tongue and not speak of my plans until necessary for logistical purposes."

He nodded gratefully to her and looked up at Charles as if to say, *See? She can be reasonable.*

So, as the months passed, she nurtured the dream inside herself, stoking the furnace with letters from Melissa, secret encouragement from Louise-Caroline, and overt excitement from Harriet. She kept her own counsel and went through dinners like this one with only part of her soul involved in any conversation.

"It's valuable work you are doing for our society," the dinner guest said with gravity. "You must be very proud and pleased."

His words snapped Louisa back from her reverie. Remembering her promises, though, she said, "It will do for now. But I don't expect I'll be a teacher forever."

Wiping his mustache with the napkin that reminded Louisa of the snow-capped Rockies, the man leaned closer. "Perhaps you would do me the honor of taking a turn about the garden with me after dinner, Miss Hovey. I find the air this time of year so refreshing."

~   ~   ~

As she brushed her hair before bed, Louisa thought about the increase in visitors the family had welcomed to the dinner table in the last few months. At least once a week, if not more, some old Regiment friend of Charles' or a working acquaintance of George's came to dine. Most were older than she; some clearly had gotten the worse end of the War with wounds and scars that had never disappeared. They were polite. They were well-mannered. They were... attentive.

Her hairbrush stopped. Why were men suddenly attentive to her? They were invariably seated next to her, even when Harriet joined them. They all seemed to want to talk to her. It wasn't like she was getting any younger—and certainly not prettier. She was

51

what she was, and though she was content with her lot, it puzzled her that it seemed enough for others now when it never had before.

After turning out the light, Louisa pulled the feather quilt over her shoulders and stared at the ceiling. But the unusual thoughts soon led to visions and dreams of a starry sky in cool, high altitudes with a bustling young city below.

CHAPTER 9

Spring 1882, Boston

My Dear Melissa:

I received your most recent letter and am grateful for all you do in Denver to promote our joint interests. I realize that setbacks will occur from time to time. You should not think this is causing me second thoughts about continuing our speculations. Thanks to your shrewd study of the market, we have already earned many times over what I initially invested, and I am not alarmed by a slight loss.

Each of your letters encouraging me to cut my ties and move immediately is more tempting than the last. I find it challenging to stay the course regarding my work at school, wishing for nothing more than to turn in my keys and give my class to someone else. However, I am built stronger than that. I believe in finishing a job unless it becomes untenable. I plan to finish the school year, gather my belongings, and book a ticket West.

At least it is not dull here this winter. My brother, Charles, has taken on a new position in his regimental club, so our table includes one or more old soldiers most evenings. Weekends include small gatherings and even dances. For staid, parsimonious Charles, this is most unusual. Yet he loves everything to do with his old command and is just doing what he can to cheer those who came out of the War worse off than he.

Did I tell you he was wounded and captured in the course of his service? He received a wound to his face at Antietam, which surely gave him a most unsettling appearance to the enemy for the rest of the War. He sustained a gunshot in the leg at Gettysburg. He was captured while part of a higher officer's staff and rescued from that situation. All this has had a profound impact on him.

His constant involvement in regimental offices and events shows me he is a backward-looking man, and I have difficulty understanding that. I have had my life wounds. I lost my mother when I was a tiny child. My father moved to St. Louis to continue his work in the carriage building trade there when I was in my early teens, and I was left here in Boston to live with my sister. I have never been a beauty and never married. Such things have caused other women to turn inward and seem to grow smaller.

I look at them as drivers that are moving me forward. My eye is on the horizon. I can't wait to see what is around the next bend in the road. I am who I am because of my past, but my future remains unwritten. I still have the pen and am determined to conclude my story satisfactorily.

I see the same attitude in you, Melissa, which is why we are so compatible. I look forward to continuing and expanding our friendship when I become a resident of Denver in just a few months. Keep an eye out for suitable lodging for me.

Fondly,
Louisa

~ ~ ~

An unseasonable burst of warm weather demanded the French windows be open from the parlor to the garden after Sunday dinner, and the scent of early flowers tickled Louisa's nose. She tuned out the chatter of the women around her as they settled into their evening amusements and awaited the men's return from their cigars and whiskey. She wondered what Denver smelled like in April and smiled secretly to herself.

When Charles led the men into the midst of the women, one moved briskly to Louisa's side. Herbert had become a regular at their table over the past months, and his attention to her was becoming noticeable. Tall and heavyset with large mutton chop whiskers, he was intelligent enough, if not quite as interesting as she'd prefer for a conversational companion.

Louisa kept her promise to Charles and George and did not speak about her plans to move to Denver, though she wished to tell everyone she met. As Herbert shyly bowed to her and leaned in to talk, she wondered what his expression would be if she suddenly blurted out her intentions.

It seemed, however, that his intentions were uppermost on his mind.

"Miss Louisa, would you do me the great honor of joining me for a turn in the garden this fine evening? I want to enjoy it before the cool of the night sets in."

Louisa was just as eager to be outside and consented to his request. He offered his arm and led her gently through the open doors. The sun had painted a splash of rose, gold, and purple across the sky while it sank into the west, and they both stopped to admire it. Then Herbert gently edged her to the stone bench at the side of the garden and urged her to sit.

Silence fell between them, and she took the opportunity to breathe deeply, trying to determine which blossom had come out in the last few days and was soaking the air with its sweet scent. Her contemplation was interrupted when he cleared his throat.

"Miss Louisa, I hope I do not startle you, but surely you must have noticed that I have a powerful desire to be in your company any opportunity I get," Herbert began, a smile quivering on his lips.

"It is an honor for me to be included in your family gatherings, and I trust that my relationship with your brother will be a mark in my favor."

Louisa wasn't sure how to respond. Be honest and say that Charles was as different from her as lavender and lye, or be polite?

Social convention won out, but she couldn't resist a little mischief.

"I am glad that you and Charles and the rest of the men from the Regiment can continue so companionably. I know you all share memories that none of us who did not fight can possibly comprehend."

"This is true, of course. But I'm more interested in seeing your family than Colonel Hovey, though he is generous in inviting me to dinner."

"We are an interesting assortment, I suppose," she smiled. "My brother-in-law George has so many stories to tell about the books he's publishing. My sister Rebecca is very sweet and brings a lightness to any table. And I must admit I do enjoy sparring verbally with George's mother from time to time."

He nodded but frowned in frustration as well.

"And I'm glad you've met my dear friend Harriet. She and I have been close since childhood when her father worked with my father in building carriages. We both teach at the Lewis School, which gives us more time together."

"She's very nice, I'm sure." He combed his hand through his side whiskers. "But Miss Louisa, I will be bold and tell you that it is you I come to see. And I hope, in a small way, that you also look forward to my visits."

Louisa had known where he was going and decided to put him out of his misery. She'd teased him long enough. The fact that he appeared not to realize it was just one more thing she found lacking in him.

"Why, that's kind of you to say. I enjoy seeing all the men from the Regiment, and you and I have had several good moments here in the garden enjoying the air."

He straightened his shoulders, appearing to draw his courage about him for one last battle. "Please do not think me rude for being forthright, Miss Louisa, but I would like to expand our relationship beyond that of dinner companions. I would like you to consider me a suitor. Your only suitor. Dare I hope that you can see me in that light?"

His question was more than Louisa bargained for this evening.

"Herbert..." she began, but he had found his courage and would not let it go.

"Oh, Louisa, please don't turn me down. There is more to me than meets the eye. I am not the most handsome man, but I am steadfast. I have built my reputation here in town as a goods trader and hope to expand my offerings and holdings through an advantageous marriage. Imagine what we could do working together. With my business acumen and your dowry, we could purchase a new property, build a proper warehouse, and capitalize on the booming trade that Boston is experiencing! I could do it with you by my side; I know I could."

Herbert's eyes sparkled, and his unconscious clasp on her hand had become slightly uncomfortable. She knew her own eyes must be glowing too, but not for the reason he hoped. She wiggled her fingers to indicate she needed a release from his pressure, but he only clung harder.

"I think there is some mistake here, Herbert," she said, puzzled. "I am just a schoolteacher. I have no money. I have no dowry. I would bring nothing but myself to a marriage if I were so inclined to enter into one—which I am not. Do you realize I will be 42 years old in a few weeks? I am certainly no beauty, and though I am interested in building my assets, it is not in trade—and certainly not in Boston—that I plan to do that."

Herbert's grasp of her hand became as slack as his jaw. He took in her words, and his eyebrows lowered most unbecomingly. He began to sputter and shake his large head. "But this is not true! I was told in no uncertain terms that there was three thousand in dowry for your hand. It would be all we need to set ourselves up very nicely."

Now, it was Louisa's turn to feel her jaw drop. "Exactly where did you hear that, Herbert? It is patently false. True, my father left me a small inheritance. But I must speak out and be plain with you. I have spent nearly all of it. Though I promised not to discuss this, it seems I must. I used it to buy land in Denver, where I intend to relocate this summer!"

The silence deepened, and Herbert's face became angry red. His mutton chops bristled and looked like they were standing at attention in indignation.

"But your brother said—" Too late, he stopped speaking. He must have been sworn to secrecy on some matters, as well. Louisa stiffened.

"Charles told you I had a three thousand dollar dowry?" she demanded.

Herbert dropped her hand and his head. "I ask your forgiveness, Miss Louisa. I have broken a confidence." He started to rise, but now she clamped a hand on his arm and forced him back down. It was that, or he would have to wrestle with her to escape, and she knew his good manners would not let that happen.

"No, Herbert. You are going to sit here and tell me what is going on. Hold nothing back. Someone has misled you; I intend to correct the situation." Pieces and memories all fell into place in her mind.

"Charles told me—told all of us—about your dowry," he sighed. He said it would be helpful to any man who could win your heart and marry you. It is common knowledge in the Regiment."

Louisa ground her teeth. She started to turn away but realized it was not Herbert who was at fault. She turned back. "As I said, you have been misled. I value your friendship, Herbert, but I have no intention of marrying, especially now that I have settled plans to move West. If this had come from anyone but Charles, I would assume it was a cruel joke. Now I see it is a well-laid plan on his part."

Not willing to concede, Herbert retook her hand, more gently this time. "I am still willing to marry you. I have asked, and my honor will not allow me to rescind the offer even if circumstances... change."

She patted his hand and, for once, felt genuine affection for him. "Don't trouble yourself, Herbert. I am not insulted. Honestly, I might have done the same thing if I were in your shoes. But you and I are headed in different directions." She tipped her head back to look at the emerging stars. "I do have one favor to ask of you, however."

"Name it, Miss Louisa. Anything."

She sat back and thought for a moment. "I know you are a kind man, Herbert. And I like you as a friend. Would you be willing to be my friend—my somewhat exclusive friend—from now until I leave for Denver? Having you fill that role would prevent any other gentlemen in the Regiment from making the same mistake. And it would make my life a little easier. I would count it a great service."

Herbert nodded sadly. "Yes, I can do that." His eyes gleamed with mischief for a moment. "In exchange, I would like to hear about your plans, why you want to relocate, and what adventures you anticipate. I could never do something like that, but thinking about it would be fun." He winked. "And again, I consider the offer still open in case, throughout our special friendship, you find you can't, after all, move across the country."

Louisa smiled and lay her hand gently on his sleeve. "Agreed."

They lingered in the garden a few more minutes, and she saw Charles passing the French doors more than once, glancing out at them. He seemed tense and overly interested in the result of their conversation. *Let him squirm a while longer! He'll be more than uncomfortable when I get done with him....*

CHAPTER 10

April 1881, Boston

Dear Louisa,

I don't need to tell you that Denver's growth continues in your (temporary!) absence. The sounds of ringing hammers and rasping saws begin at dawn and end each day at sunset.

The only thing that does not change is your beloved mountains, other than to shrug off their snowy mantles and fill the streams with runoff. Inevitably, some of that ends up in Denver, making a mess of the roads that cross the riverbed.

I paused my land projects briefly to find you a place to live when you arrive in a few months. I am pleased to tell you that you now have an address in Denver!

587 Champa, Denver, Colorado

It is nothing palatial but an entirely respectable suite of rooms near mine. I have told the woman who owns the house to store anything that arrives for you in case you begin sending some of your goods ahead of your move. This will make traveling so much easier.

Don't worry that you owe me anything. I used some of your funds to pay advanced rent so you can start your new life free and clear. In time, you can see which way the city is moving and consider a different home, but now you have a place to lay your head and plant your feet.

Anticipating your arrival,
Melissa

Louisa ran her finger over the address in the letter. It made everything so much more real, and she knew Melissa had intended it to anchor her to Denver and keep her from backing out. There was no chance of that, however. She was going, and nothing would stop her.

She folded the letter carefully and stowed it in a hidden compartment at the bottom of her traveling bag. No need to have Charles fretting and fuming if he came across it somewhere in the house. It had been an inspired idea to have Melissa direct all correspondence for her to Harriet. She could always tell by the sparkle in her friend's eyes when they met that she'd received another to pass on.

I'll miss Harriet terribly. But still. . . 587 Champa. I'm going home!

~ ~ ~

Herbert stood at his table as Louisa and Harriet entered the tearoom. They'd fallen into a pattern of getting together with Harriet filling the role of ostensible chaperone at least once a week over the past month. Louisa thought the need for someone to watch

61

over a courting couple should end well before 40, but she needed the meetings to accomplish her plans.

"Did you purchase anything nice today?" he asked, gesturing at the parcels they carried bearing the names of modest but quality shops around the city.

"Yes, a wonderful coat, which I'm sure I'll need, and some other things I'd ordered previously and had adjusted to fit." Louisa lowered herself into a seat, and they stacked their packages on an extra chair at the table.

"I've had a letter too," said Harriet. A waiter swept to the table and placed additional teacups, plates, and sandwiches for the two women. When Herbert nodded to him, he faded away again.

"What's the news," he asked.

"All the other packages have arrived safe and sound," said Louisa, "and so I can travel lightly. I'm so excited," she smiled. When she did, her grey eyes glowed, and her cheeks reddened. Herbert seemed to appreciate both.

"The weather has begun to warm a bit," Louisa continued. "My friend Melissa said that much of the spring snow melt has ended, and the streets are becoming passable again. I can enjoy a full summer and autumn in Denver before bracing for the winter. How interesting that will be!"

Herbert helped himself to a lemon cake drizzled with frosting and topped with a fresh strawberry. After he had swallowed and sipped some tea, he wiped his mouth. "Over the past weeks, you have described Denver to me and shown me so many newspaper articles about it that I must confess it has a certain allure. Not for me, of course," he held up a hand quickly and dropped it, "but I can see how it captured your imagination in the first place.

He coughed and blushed. "And this cloak-and-dagger activity has been most stimulating," he admitted. "I almost ran straight into Charles at the post office the other day. I'd just sent the package, and I saw him come in. I knew he'd ask what I was there for, so I turned like a small boy and darted down the back corridor to escape. Most unseemly but rather exciting."

Louisa smiled indulgently. Herbert had grown on her. It was not enough to make her stay in Boston, but he'd certainly become a friend to her and, by extension, to Harriet. She knew they'd continue to collaborate after she was gone. It was a comfort she was not leaving them both without a confidante.

"587 Champa is filling up! It's a good thing you plan to travel soon," Harriet said, choosing a cranberry scone and adding extra cream to her fresh cup of tea. Around them, the conversations at other tables created a veil of privacy.

"I've left my old dresses and garments in my room. It should take Charles at least a day to realize I am gone. I'm still trying to figure out when I will leave. He's planned a special dinner with the Regimental officers and the doctor, as well as other social events. He still hopes I'll forget Denver since I've not mentioned it in months."

Herbert sat up suddenly. "What did you say?"

Louisa started to repeat herself, but he cut her off. "This is very serious, Louisa. It helps me understand a conversation I overheard in the smoking room at the Regimental Club. It had to do with a newspaper article from Chicago." His bushy eyebrows seemed to quiver and chase each other across his face.

Used to his habit of drifting off in mid-conversation, Louisa put down her cup. "Herbert. What do you mean? Don't stop like that and leave us on tenterhooks!"

Herbert shook his head to return to reality and leaned back in his chair. "Some men were speaking about women, as they often do. But a specific case was brought up in which a woman named Elizabeth Packard was sent to an insane asylum for three years because she argued with her husband about theology and did not obey him in other areas of domestic life."

Louisa and Harriet exchanged confused looks.

"The point they were making was that some women today seem to feel they are better than men, or at least equal, and they go so far as to get an education and make their own choices about important things."

Louisa growled. "An educated woman is a wonderful thing."
"I think we all agree on that. What has this article to do with
Louisa?" asked Harriet.

Herbert looked at Louisa. "Choices. . . like uprooting their lives
and moving to Denver." He put his napkin down carefully next to
his plate. "It wasn't the discussion of Mrs. Packard that bothered
me. Immediately after, Charles suddenly asked the Regimental
doctor to dinner—and extended the invitation to some other men.
In Mrs. Packard's case, her husband used a doctor's opinion to
adjudge his wife insane. That was all it took to lock her up."

There was a horrified silence at the table. When Louisa lifted her
cup to her lips, she realized her hand shook just the tiniest bit.

"Surely you don't think Charles. . . that George. . . that they'd try
this tactic to keep me here?" she asked.

"Not George," Harriet said hastily, defending Louisa's brother-
in-law. "He's too fine a man for that. But Charles? Yes, I can see
him mulling over the possibilities. He could startle you by breaking
his rule on talking about your plans and getting you to go on and on
about Denver with the doctor listening intently." She turned to
Louisa. "You must admit, my dear, that it sounds like a crazy plan
to most people. Once you are pronounced insane, getting you free
again will take a massive amount of effort. The stigma would
follow you, too."

Herbert's expression darkened as he nodded. "When is this
dinner to happen? I've lost track. I receive so many invitations in
the role of your suitor."

"Saturday after next," Louisa whispered. Her heart pounded,
and she felt as if dark, dank walls were closing in on her. Until now,
moving to Denver had been a giddy dream—a fun plan that they
executed by shipping her new clothes and other items west without
the family being any the wiser. Suddenly, it was serious. And
dangerous.

Practical Harriet took the lead in the crisis. "Right, you two. Five
days from today, we will meet at the art museum. They have a new
exhibit on then. We must each devise a plan to keep Louisa from

this terrible fate. We'll compare plans, select the best one, and then work out the details. There's a terrace at the museum where we can sit and talk. Being gone for hours will not seem odd if we are viewing the paintings."

A tiny ray of light pierced the fearful darkness Louisa sensed around herself. She reached out and clasped Harriet's hand. "Thank you, my dear friend. And you, Herbert." She put her hand on his sleeve as well. "A problem is just a challenge to overcome. Let's find the way through this one."

"Oh, Louisa! You are such a treasure," Herbert said. He lifted her hand and kissed it.

~   ~   ~

The council of war commenced when they found a comfortable corner of the museum terrace to linger over coffee and cakes. Harriet withdrew a tablet and pen from her reticule to take notes. Louisa looked tired. Weariness beyond her age dragged at her shoulders and slowed her steps. The meeting with her friends had filled all her thoughts since the revelation of her brother's potential treachery the week before. Each day, she pondered. Each night, she tossed and turned. Finally, she had her supporters around her to help find answers.

She had considered bringing Louise-Caroline for support and help, but she was too close to Charles. Knowing her fiery spirit, she might confront her husband and ruin everything. It would be best for her sister-in-law to be unaware of the plan until it was too late to stop it.

"The way I see it, there are a few possible campaign modes here," said Herbert. "The first is that we can announce our engagement."

Louisa choked on her coffee, and Harriet stared at him open-mouthed with her pen in the air.

"Please let me finish," he said, waving his hands. "I don't mean it would be real. But it might be enough to stall Charles while he waits to see how it plays out. That would give you time to make your departure."

"Hmmm. I can see how that would draw Charles up short," said Louisa.

"But aren't there certain legal ramifications to announcing a betrothal?" said Harriet. "It could add difficulties to what is already a tangled situation." They all nodded.

Herbert put down his cup. "The Second option is to go in the dead of night. Leave your home and go to the train station.

Obviously, before the evening of the dinner."

They considered this proposal in silence. Finally, Louisa shook her head. "It makes me seem like a criminal."

"Knowing Charles, he would have someone after her like a shot to bring her back and confine her for her 'safety' if she did that," said Harriet. "We need something that gives Louisa time to get to Denver with minimal fuss. Once there, she'd be under entirely different state laws and probably be safe. She already knows some prominent people there."

They poured more coffee, consumed more cookies and cakes, and pondered the situation. They paid no heed to the beautiful day or the art on exhibit.

Suddenly, Harriet sat up. "I feel ill!"

Louisa and Herbert both turned to her and reached out their hands. "What's wrong, dear?" Louisa said. "Do we need to get a cab?"

Harriet laughed. "No, sillies, I am going to feel ill. Very, very ill. On Saturday."

Herbert and Louisa exchanged looks, and Harriet began scribbling notes.

CHAPTER 11

June 10, 1882, Boston

11:00 a.m.

Dearest Louisa,

I woke with a dreadful head this morning, feeling progressively worse as the day advances. Perhaps it is just the sadness about the loss of my father. It just doesn't seem real to me. I did not expect it to affect me physically, but I feel depleted.

Harriet

11:20 a.m.

My dear,

Do you need anything? I will miss you at the Regimental dinner this evening, but everyone completely understands your situation. We must respect a loss like yours. I know if my father were still alive, he would mourn the loss of his carriage craftsman friend Ambrose almost more than if I were to pass away. Take care of yourself, my friend.

Louisa

2:45 p.m.

Miss Hovey,

Miss Davenport is worsening, and her brother has sent for the doctor. I wanted you to know. She said you are not to come, as she does not want you to catch what she might have, lest it be more than just feeling low.

Lucinda (housemaid)

4:15 p.m.

Miss Hovey,

The doctor is concerned for Miss Davenport and wishes her to have someone sit with her for the night. The current household situation entirely debilitates her mother, so I thought you would want to be aware.

He does not feel it is contagious, but she needs someone. I know she wants me to ask you.

Lucinda

4:40 p.m.

Louise-Caroline,

In haste, Harriet is worse, and the doctor has requested that someone sit with her overnight. I am so sorry I will miss the lovely party, but I must go to her. I will let you know how she fares in the morning.

Louisa

5:30 p.m.

Dear Herbert,

I do not want you to be startled by my absence this evening. Harriet fell ill this morning, and the doctor came to see her. I will be sitting with her all night to assure myself that she gets better.
I looked forward to dancing this evening, but I know you understand. We can have a long chat on Thursday when we attend the new exhibit at the Athenaeum. I will have the book on architecture I borrowed from there with me at Harriet's bedside to keep me occupied when she sleeps. There is much we can discuss in it.

Fondly,
Louisa

~ ~ ~

Harriet appeared at the station veiled and in mourning dress. Louisa wore a large hat, hoping to avoid recognition by anyone who might know her. Sounds of train whistles and hurrying feet surrounded them.

Since Louisa had shipped all her goods ahead, she stood with her heart beating fast and a small travel bag at her feet. Harriet

69

embraced her, and it was almost more than she could do to break away. So many memories! Even the tangling of the hats wasn't enough to make Louisa smile.

Harriet sensed her emotion at once. Her gloved hand slipped a crackling envelope into Louisa's pocket, and she patted it affectionately. Despite her pain, she blinked back tears to be sure Louisa would get on the train.

"Now, you go out there and make a name for yourself! Don't you even think about us for at least a month while you get settled. But then I expect regular letters telling me the latest adventures you've gotten yourself into!" Her bracing words straightened Louisa's back and brought a smile to her face.

"You know I could not have done this without you," she said. Harriet's eyes twinkled. "Of course, you couldn't. I was always the one in our friendship who had the best ideas. And it's been fun planning this one." She glanced at the big station clock and then back to Louisa. "I refuse to cry. I will save that for when I return to my 'sick bed' to await the inevitable visit from Charles."

"He's going to be horrible," Louisa warned.

"He has no right to be. Louisa, you're 42 years old. Go be who you want to be!"

The whistles began to blow more urgently, loudspeakers made announcements, and with a last hug, Louisa climbed onto the train. When she looked out the window, Harriet was gone. She was grateful; it made it easier for them both.

A few minutes later, the conductor passed along the train's length, and the wheels began to move. The tension in Louisa's body relaxed fractionally. There was still a long way to go before she was safe. She dipped into her coat pocket to distract herself and extracted the letter Harriet had deposited there. With surprise, she saw it was from Herbert.

Oh, Louisa!

I am feeling quite as ill as Harriet is supposed to be, knowing that by the time you read this note, you will be gone from my life. I have enjoyed spending time with you, exploring the cultural aspects of our city, visiting friends, and hearing your unique thoughts about life. You have made my world bigger by having you in it, and I will be desolate without you. I won't have to act that part at the dinner this evening!

I trust our plans are moving ahead since I received your note about Harriet. I know that as much as she is delighting in this affair, her sense of personal loss tempers her enthusiasm. I will call upon her later in the week to ascertain her actual state of mind and retrieve your borrowed book. Harriet and I will try to hold each other up as we get used to life without you. As exciting as it has been to plan your great escape, I am only now beginning to feel the inevitable hole you leave in my life.

Write and tell me all your new adventures!

You know how I feel,
Herbert

Louisa held Herbert's letter and read it a second time while sipping tea in the dining car, trying hard not to let a tear slip. He had indeed been a friend to her in her months of need, and she would miss him greatly. Leaving hurt her more than she expected.

At least I didn't hurt him unawares. He knew this day was coming.

The wheels clacked beneath her, and she started to let herself believe she was really on her way, Louisa took up her pen to draft a telegram to the one person who was as excited as she was.

TELEGRAM

JUNE 10
TO: MELISSA HOTCHKISS, DENVER

BOARDED TRAIN THIS EVENING [STOP] **ARRIVE DENVER THREE DAYS** [STOP] **FINALLY** [STOP] **LOUISA**

She splurged on that last word to give herself courage. It had been so long since she'd breathed the air of the Rockies. Now, she was racing toward Albany, where she would send the telegram. Then, it was on to Chicago and westward to pick up the Transcontinental Railroad and, finally, the branch line that went to Denver.

Each mile made her feel safer. She knew Charles could still try to claw her back if he realized she was gone. He had connections. He even knew Pinkerton men and could set them to follow her. Speed and distance were her greatest friends. Once in Denver, she would disappear into her nondescript boarding house and wait for the storm to pass.

No doubt her brother would rage about her missing his Regimental dinner after all his planning. The doctor would be ready to evaluate her state of mental capacity and perhaps even have arranged where he would have her transported directly from the table! It had happened to women before.

After a day or two (oh, she hoped for two!) Charles would no doubt arrive at George and Rebecca's house and demand to look at her room out of suspicion. There, he would find a closet with familiar garments, accessories on the dressing table, and even an open book by the bedside. Not satisfied, he would go to Harriet's home and demand to know where Louisa had gone. It would take him a while to work out that she had slowly and methodically replaced every item in her room with new ones and shipped them to Denver.

When the explosion happened, she expected to hear it all the way out West.

She regretted being unable to tell Louise-Caroline the final plans and their timing. When she last saw her sister-in-law on Friday, Louisa gave her a fiercer, longer-than-usual parting hug. Always perceptive, Louise-Caroline pulled back and eyed her carefully.

Louisa chose to believe that she realized the departure was imminent. But she left her in the dark to face her husband's wrath truthfully and say she knew nothing.

The last class with her students earlier in the week had been hectic, but they remembered she had said she would not be back. They asked her if it were true, and she chose to hedge.

"We'll just have to see, won't we?"

They groaned. Their teacher often dragged out answers to get them to pay attention.

The tea had gone cold while she mused, but Louisa was too tired from a day of subterfuge and activity to order another. She gathered her letter from Herbert and her handbag, then went down the car to her sleeping cubicle.

No more economy travel for her. She was going home to Denver first class.

PART 2

CHAPTER 12

June 13, 1882, Denver, Colorado

The worst thing about traveling by train, even when she had splurged on a sleeper, was the grubbiness that Louisa felt as Union Station filled her window. She rewashed her hands, checked her hair in the tiny mirror above the basin, and gathered up her travel bag. A last look around assured her she'd left nothing behind except the hideous hat she'd used to cover her identity.

No more hiding now. I'm free, and I'm going to live like it.

People jostled in the corridor as they moved eagerly toward the exits. Louisa joined them, her eyes longing for her mountains, her ears ringing with all the sounds of a journey's end. The corners of her mouth curved upward in anticipation.

The first thing she saw was the wide eyes of Melissa Hotchkiss. An even wider hug enveloped her.

"Oh, Louisa! I knew you could do it! I'm so happy to see you. Welcome home!"

The reception bowled Louisa over. Impulsively, she dropped her bag and wrapped Melissa in an embrace of her own. Then she stepped back.

"I'm grimy and messy and completely exhausted. Don't soil your pretty dress on me," she admonished. Melissa only laughed.

"I bet that's the tone of voice you used on those disobedient little boys in Boston. Well, it won't work here, missy." To prove her point, she hugged Louisa again.

When they pulled apart, Melissa took Louisa's arm in hers and snatched up her travel bag with her free hand. "Right this way, madam. My carriage awaits. The next stop is 587 Champa!"

Louisa was relieved. She'd expected to have to get a cab. Her exhaustion made walking a chore, and having someone like Melissa take over felt good. She'd re-familiarize herself with Denver in the coming days, but today was a day to be coddled and welcomed and have someone make much of her. It was so good to be accepted!

They moved along the platform, across the enormous echoing entry hall, and onto the bustling street. Melissa waved, and her coachman flicked his whip gently to urge the horses forward. He hopped down, took Louisa's bag, put it inside, and helped both women board.

"You won't believe how Denver has changed since you were here. If you stand still long enough, a building will sprout under you, I swear. It's like the whole city is in a race to make things and mine things and fill up with more people who want to do more of the same."

"So your letters said. I have been looking forward to seeing it all. And now that I never have to leave again, it will make it much more exciting."

"The only way you leave Denver is to visit somewhere else. Then you come high-tailing it back here again. Oh, I've so much to tell you." Melissa looked into Louisa's tired eyes. "But for today, all you will do is explore your new rooms and maybe shove a few boxes and trunks around. Don't even think about unpacking. Give yourself some time to relax."

Louisa's head fell back onto the upholstery, and she sighed. "I won't even have the energy to unpack this bag," she patted her traveler, "much less start opening other things. Once I leave this carriage, I don't want to move for at least three days. I still feel the vibration of the trains all through me."

The view out the window was everything Melissa had described and more. There wasn't a single person who was not carrying something, building something, or otherwise hurrying to and fro. At the moment, it only increased Louisa's weariness. They rode silently the rest of the way, finally pulling up in front of an attractive two-story home with a porch and bright red shutters accenting the windows. Louisa drank it in.

The driver handed them down, and both women moved up the sidewalk. A jovial-faced older woman with a plump body and a flour-spattered apron opened the door.

"Miss Hotchkiss. How good to see you again. And this must be Miss Hovey." The woman wiped her hands quickly on the apron. "Forgive my appearance, but it's baking day. I'm Mrs. Burnett. Won't you please come in?"

The warm smell of yeast and sugar enfolded them when they stepped inside. A parlor opened to the right, a dining room to the left, and stairs led straight up. Down a hallway next to the stairs, Louisa heard the sound of young voices and pans clattering. She liked the place immediately.

"I hope you had a good trip," Mrs. Burnett said, taking the travel bag from the carriage driver and turning toward the stairs. "I know you want to see your rooms. Let's go right up. You can explore the rest of the house later."

Suddenly, the stairs looked too tall to climb. Louisa put her hand on the banister and stopped, her face lifted toward the second floor. Sensing her friend's true fatigue, Melissa took her arm. Together, they followed the landlady up the carpeted stairs to a suite of rooms painted in a pale yellow with white lace curtains and dark wood furniture.

There were two rooms. One held a bed, bedside table, dresser, and wardrobe, as well as a round table and comfortable chair near the window. The other served as a private parlor where Louisa could have friends visit. Familiar boxes that had made their way from Boston to Denver surreptitiously over the preceding months carpeted the floor.

Melissa again took charge.

"Mrs. Burnett, I am going to leave Louisa in your charge. I know she's as tired as anybody can be, and she's been through a lot getting here. Would you be so good as to check in on her at dinner time and be sure she's still breathing? I think there's a nap in her immediate future."

Mrs. Burnett chuckled. "I'll do better than that. I'll bring up a tray with her dinner on it, and if she's asleep, I'll leave it on the table. I think a cup of tea, a sandwich, and some of Molly's freshly baked cookies are needed right now."

Louisa stood still as the conversation and plans flowed around her. Then, she slowly lowered herself to sit on the edge of the bed—which was blessedly firm and comfortable.

"I'll have Katie bring up a pitcher of nice hot water," the landlady said, gesturing to the bowl on the dresser and lifting the large ewer to take with her. "You just settle in, Miss Hovey." She nodded briefly, turned, and left the room.

Louisa was sure Melissa must have said something before she left but later could not recall it. When Katie arrived with steaming water, soap, and towels, she was still sitting on the bed. Mrs. Burnett accompanied her, put a plate and cup of tea on the table, and then left as quickly as she'd come.

With a mighty effort, Louisa stood and began to undress. She took bites of the sandwich and sips of the tea as she worked. The cookies vanished somehow. Ten minutes later, having bathed and put on her travel nightgown, she slid between cool sheets. Her eyes were not fully closed before she lost contact with her new world.

~   ~   ~

June 14, 1882, Denver

My Dear Harriet:

I am sure this letter will cross paths with yours somewhere in the middle of the country, but I want to let you know I have arrived safely and all is well.

Melissa met me on the train platform and brought me to my delightful first home! I wish you could see it. It is just to your taste, as it is mine. The landlady is a cheerful soul who runs her house efficiently but with great kindness. The maid (Katie) and the assistant cook (Molly) are Irish. They are very young, adore Mrs. Burnett, and serve her guests with smiles and good nature. (I need to find out their stories. I can't believe they traveled from Ireland at their age and somehow fetched up here.)

Why did I never insist that Charles let me paint my room yellow? To wake up in a new, vibrant city with the sun streaming in, a view of the mountains, and a golden glow on the walls is beyond anything I can describe. I bounced out of bed this morning the moment I opened my eyes. I opened all my boxes and put my things where I wanted them. It's funny, but I decided to put them in places unlike where they were "back home" just to distinguish in my head that I am here at last. I know you are now laughing at me.

My little investment in land has grown considerably under Melissa's care. Thanks to her, I don't have to worry about money for now. I know she has much to teach me about business, but we will explore Denver together in the meantime, and she will introduce me to her friends. I hope to build a coterie of like-minded people, so I don't just pine away from missing you and—surprisingly—Herbert. We did have a grand time making this a reality. I wish I could return the favor to each of you so you could achieve your dreams, too.

This house is in a part of town where many buildings are going up (though I could say that of anywhere in Denver. The city is exploding in all directions). It includes an airy parlor downstairs, a

81

dining room, a well-equipped kitchen, and a vegetable garden in the backyard. Mrs. Burnett's rooms are also on the ground floor, and the two maids share a small room on the second floor with me.

My rooms include a bedroom and a sunny sitting room where I can have visitors. A fresh breeze is blowing through the open windows, lifting the lace curtains fancifully. I keep them open all day and stare at the mountains whenever I tire of unpacking.

Tomorrow, I will go out with Melissa to see what is going on in the city. We'll visit some land that I might purchase. We will meet people and go to dinner, and I will be happy.

I await your first letter as I am dying to hear what happened when Charles realized I had gone. Do I need to be worried about Pinkertons? Or worse, Charles himself? I know you will tell me all about it.

I miss you,
Louisa

A rested and optimistic Louisa stepped out of the boarding house to greet Melissa the next day. Her new dress, a mix of blue and purple details, made her feel like a freshly blooming spring flower. Her friend's approval confirmed her decision back in Boston to dispense with old clothes and only ship new ones.

"Now that's more like it!" Melissa laughed. "When I left you a few days ago, I thought you would be in bed for a week. And I feared you'd regret making this move."

Louisa shook her head vehemently. "I just needed to recover. It was more of an upheaval than I'd anticipated. But now I have put all my things away, and Mrs. Burnett's cooking and ministrations have restored my spirits. I'm ready to begin my new life." She touched Melissa's arm with a warm clasp. "Thank you for all your encouragement and help."

"It was my pleasure from start to finish," Melissa replied. "And it's only going to get better. When we first met, I knew we'd be fast friends, and now we'll pick right up where we left off." She gestured to her carriage and driver. "Shall we go?"

Positioning herself at a window, Louisa leaned forward to examine everything they passed while Melissa kept up a running commentary on the changes Denver had undergone in just a year. Whole new sections of land were opening up for homes and streets, trade was booming, and the mines continued to fill the town with ore and miners ready to spend their wages.

"They call it a Boom Town with good reason," Melissa said. "I got you a room a bit off from the rowdier parts of town where gunshots are a regular occurrence." They both laughed.

The carriage drew up in front of the multi-story brick facade of the bustling Windsor Hotel. Carriages of all descriptions rolled past or paused to discharge passengers. Louisa turned a curious face to Melissa, raising one eyebrow in silent question.

"I thought it would be nice to start with a lovely tea so you can tell me the whole story of your escape from Boston. Then, we'll begin your exploration of Denver and all it holds. How does that sound?"

"Wonderful," Louisa sighed. "I have pictured the dining room of this hotel in my head for a year and longed to see it again. It's the perfect place to start."

The *maitre d'hotel* proved his impressive acuity when he bowed to them as they entered the opulent dining room. "Miss Hotchkiss, always a pleasure to see you. And... Miss Hovey. Welcome back."

He directed them to a table near the windows screened from other tables by tall potted palms and seated each lady in turn.

Melissa ordered tea, cakes, and sandwiches and then sat back with a happy sigh. "You can't do Denver if you don't start with the Windsor." She glanced around the room, taking inventory of the other people dining there, and then leaned toward Louisa. "Do you recognize the man over my right shoulder?" she asked softly.

Louisa studied him. Then her brow cleared, and she said, "Mr. Brown! How could I forget the source of our first successful venture together?" Melissa beamed at her.

83

"Precisely. He is quite a prominent man in Denver now, and it is good that you have a facility for faces and names. The key to becoming part of society is recognizing people and getting them to recognize you and think well of you. You learned that lesson well in Boston, I see."

"Though I taught school for a living and didn't have a very active social life, I lived with my sister and brother-in-law. He is a publisher and often brings interesting and famous people home to dinner. My brother, Charles, was a Regimental officer in the War and also kept up those contacts. I and my friend Harriet were added to the table when he needed additional ladies."

"Ah, Harriet. How is she? I enjoyed our clandestine correspondence through her. Sometimes, she slipped in an encouraging note along with your letters. I believe I would like her."

"You would. She has the fierce loyalty of a lion and the soul of a poet." Louisa paused. "I miss her greatly and am anxious to receive a report from her about what happened after I left."

When the tea arrived, they both indulged, enjoying the delicate pastries and savory sandwiches while sipping from beautiful china cups and laughing together over the steaming pot.

"From what I gather, it was quite a narrow escape," Melissa said, finally redirecting the conversation back to their previous topic.

With a nod, Louisa blotted her lips with the snowy white napkin and sat back. "I wasn't sure I'd have the nerve to carry it out. I'd worked myself into such a state over Charles' potential reaction that it almost seemed easier to stay where I was."

Melissa's eyebrows went up, and her eyes widened in shock.

"But then I thought of all the parcels I'd shipped West, all the work you'd done to increase my holdings—not to mention finding me the perfect place to live—and I realized I was already well across the starting line. There was nothing to do but run for the finish."

After another sip of fresh tea, Louisa began her story.

CHAPTER 13

June 20, 1882, Denver

The letter was on the hall table when Louisa entered the house, tired but jubilant after a day of walking and riding around the city and studying its growth.

Darling Louisa!

Since I have not heard any rumors about Pinkertons dragging you back from the trains, I must assume that you are now safely ensconced at 587 Champa. I expect your first letter today or tomorrow, but I cannot wait to write.

Our ruse lasted until Sunday evening—just a day after you left—when Charles, as predicted, paid a call at your sister's home and demanded to see you. Bewildered, Rebecca said you were still tending to me in my "illness." Charles went to your room and came away puzzled. (I have this from the maid, a cousin of my Lucinda.)

His next stop was here, of course. His temper is something he needs to control. He stamped and shouted, and at one moment, I thought he'd raise his hand to me. I sat quietly in my chair in the parlor and waited him out. Finally, the question came.

"I demand that you tell me where Louisa is. I assume she is somewhere in this house?"

"No," I said (I admit, a bit smugly), "you assume wrong. She should be somewhere near the Nebraska border by now.

You're right. When he gets angry, his mustache fluffs!

"I hold you responsible for this fiasco by stoking her irrational ideas and helping her do idiotic things!" he shouted, waving his finger under my nose. He fluffed at me again. "If possible, I will bring charges against you for this preposterous behavior."

At that point, I'd had enough.

"Oh really? What charges would those be? The crime of friendship? The unlawful well-wishing of my 42-year-old life-long companion when she left this area to live elsewhere? The unforgivable act of circumventing your efforts to control her against her will? Which of those do you think will stand up in court?"

He fluffed again! And he even growled.

"You haven't heard the last of this," he said as he snatched up his hat and exited the room most rudely. (I should be keeping my own list of social crimes.)

Herbert (who sends his great affection and admiration to you) said that your disappearance was all the talk of the Regimental Club. Fortunately, cooler heads than Charles' were present, and they explained to him that you were not only out of his reach but also in a place with different laws and customs. After that, he had nothing left to say and pouted throughout the evening until one of his friends sent him home.

So, my dear, you can believe yourself well and truly liberated. Oh, Louisa, I am so proud of you! But you must promise to write to me regularly and share your ongoing adventures. I know you will have many.

How is Melissa? If her letters are anything to go by, I know I would like her in person. Please tell her she must not cease to write to me because you are now in Denver. You know I am a faithful and eager correspondent with all my friends.

Take care, and go look at something amazing today just for me.

Affectionately,
Harriet

Something amazing. Louisa let her mind linger on the many sights she'd seen just that day that would fit the bill. Long parades of mule-drawn wagons came down from the mountains on their way to the smelting factories on the south side of town. Dainty beribboned little girls and fiercely combed boys followed their mothers as they went to and from school. Vast piles of bricks that would almost magically transform into sturdy buildings very soon.

And the mountains. Invariably, the mountains towering to the west beckoned her to make a closer visit. She made herself a promise she would do so before the month was out.

The most amazing thing she'd seen was the ledger of land purchases and sales that Melissa brought with her one morning. They sat in Louisa's cozy parlor upstairs, and the kitchen girls supplied them with tea and cookies during their meeting.

The size of the ledger took Louisa's breath away. "Why, there are over 100 transactions here!" she exclaimed as she turned the pages. Name after name, land description after land description, blurred as she tried to grasp what her friend had accomplished.

"It's kind of like an addiction, I think," Melissa laughed. "Once I got some land," she pointed to the very first transaction from 1876, "I felt so empowered. It was something tangible that no one could take from me. I walked that land repeatedly and dreamed of what I'd do with it. It came to me through my father's will."

Louisa moved her eyes to the following few lines, trying to make sense of the progression.

"It wasn't even mine, but it took me a while to realize that. My father owed money on it. It was a Trust Deed."

Louisa held her questions, trusting the answers would become clear eventually.

"Three years later, I sold it!" She pointed to the lines that recorded the details about a piece of land that had moved from her hand to someone else. Her finger pointed further along the line to the show information stating that the purchase had released sections of the land from a mortgage. "You see, by selling it, I was able to pay off the debt. And then some. So, I bought more land and began dividing it and selling it off. It got to be a game for me." She ran a finger down the page almost affectionately.

"You mean your first piece generated funds to begin buying and selling. . . all of this?" Louisa saw the logic of it and marveled at Melissa's skill.

"Exactly! Buy a big piece for a set price. Divide it up and sell each piece for more than its share of the bigger piece's price. Do it over and over. It's fun."

Louisa continued to study the ledger.

"Are you looking for your land in here?" Melissa gave her a wry smile.

"Well, I assume mine is just a piece or two of paper."

"You'd be wrong, my friend." She pointed to several transactions, far more than Louisa could believe. "Your first one turned into these. . . and these and these. You currently have several tracts that are prime for dividing and selling for homes. I've primarily focused on the Hunt Addition and the Park Avenue Addition because they are in the path of the current development swath."

"These all have your name on them," Louisa said cautiously. She was immensely grateful to Melissa but wanted to be sure she had her own holdings.

"You signed that agreement saying I could buy and sell in your name? It made it much easier to get business done quickly when you were still in Boston. I would be happy to begin putting them in your name, or you can take over your own buying and selling after I give you some instruction."

Louisa sipped tea, nibbled a buttery shortbread cookie, and considered her options. Melissa gave her space to consider her options.

"I would like to learn more about what you're doing and how you do it. But I would like to continue to have you act as my agent. You have made a name for yourself in Denver land transactions, which has to carry some weight in negotiations. I also would prefer my brother not to be able to trace what I am doing should he decide to attempt that. Is that agreeable to you? We'll have the same terms as the agreement I signed last year."

Impressed by Louisa's insightful evaluation of the situation, Melissa nodded and put out her hand. "Agreed." They shook over the teapot and then continued examining the transaction ledger in greater detail.

~ ~ ~

Melissa fulfilled her promise from their first outing by nudging Louisa into Denver society. They developed a routine week by week.

Mornings were for exploring potential land to purchase or selling some that had become of interest to another party. Afternoons were for visiting. Melissa seemed to know everyone of consequence and assiduously introduced Louisa to her friends. Evenings were for attending plays and concerts or other entertainments.

Louisa loved it all.

April 5, 1887

Dear Harriet,

I know you have grown weary of my relocating here in Denver, but I'm seeking a place to park myself for good. Though the various locations have been nice enough, I've still felt like a newcomer and almost a visitor.

At last, I've found a place to live that suits my need for proximity to Melissa and what was going on in Denver. So, on top of deleting Champa and De Forest Place from your address book, you can now also strike through Parkinson. At least for the foreseeable future, I will be living at 1561 Cleveland Place. It's taken me until age 47 to finally have a home of which I feel proud and in charge.

Last week, despite the hectic activity of moving, I returned to my favorite picnic place in the Rockies once again just to restore my soul for a moment. I had Ralph take me in his cab once more and spent a few hours near the stream. It washes away my stress every time I am there. Could there be anything better than having such a place within reach?

Your note about Herbert's stroke has left me reeling. We have exchanged a few letters over the years, and I have always felt we are good friends. Is there nothing that doctors can do for him? I imagine some of the wounds he received in the War left him prone to all manner of things as he got older. Please give him my best when you visit.

And speaking of visiting, have you given up on a plan to visit me here? I can't tell you how glorious it would be to take you around Denver and show you everything I have grown to know and love. Melissa also sends her encouragement. And now that I have a proper home, I can host you here. We could return to our young girlhoods and whisper silly thoughts late into the evenings, wake at dawn to clatter down the stairs and out the door, and not return until dusk.

Do think about it. If funds are an issue, you only have to say so. I have more than enough.

Picturing you here,
Louisa

CHAPTER 14

1888, Denver

"That will be fine, Ingrid," Louisa said as she returned the proposed menu to her housekeeper. "I hope we won't have trouble getting fresh vegetables this time." She frowned at the memory of her dinner's poor presentation six months ago. "I want everything perfect for my dear friend's visit."

"I've spoken to the grocer's man, and he's assured me there will be no problems." Irene folded the menu into her pocket and turned to go, a slight rosy stain on her cheeks.

A wry smile crossed Louisa's face. "So you've been talking to that young man again, have you? What did you say his name is?"

"Ernest, Miss Hovey." The blush deepened.

Louisa sat back in her chair and enjoyed seeing her otherwise serene housekeeper befuddled. After a turbulent time of missed deliveries and inferior quality, she'd decided to change grocers, and the benefits had extended beyond just the food. Ingrid had commented on the delivery man's looks from the first day he arrived.

"One of these days, I'll be downstairs when he arrives so I can look at him too," she teased gently. I need to keep an eye on you. I can't afford to have you running off to get married. I depend on you too much."

"Oh, Miss Hovey!" Ingrid put both her hands to her flaming cheeks and shook her head. "I am not interested in leaving your service and this grand house. Maybe someday you'll hire a gardener I take a fancy to, and we can both stay here."

Louisa laughed. "But in the meantime, passing the time of day with this. . . Ernest will do, eh?"

Ingrid shook her head, knowing her employer liked to pull her leg gently from time to time, and retreated to the kitchen to deal with the upcoming party preparations. Her mistress had been urging her friend from back East to visit for so long, and it was good to see her mood lift as she contemplated the arrival.

Days of polishing every wood surface, scrubbing all the linens, taking down and washing the curtains before rehanging them, and a million other tasks left everyone in the house tired but triumphant. Louisa stood in the foyer, thanked them for their efforts, smoothed her summer yellow dress once more, and went down the steps to the carriage.

The usual whistles blew at the station, steam gushed from engines, people shouted, cabbies maneuvered to attract passengers, and Louisa's heart flew. Six years. It had been six years since she'd seen Harriet, and she danced from foot to foot to watch the incoming trains. At last, the branch train from the Transcontinental line pulled in.

Porters immediately began opening carriage doors, lowering stairs, and handing out passengers. Louisa felt her heart speed, and tears sprang to her eyes. The fog of anticipation thickened to the point that she almost didn't see Harriet when she turned to look around. But a delighted shout and a raised hand told her all she needed to know. They rushed to each other and embraced.

"Oh, Louisa! I can't believe it! This is amazing!" Harriet said when she pulled back from Louisa's embrace.

"That you're finally here?"

"No, that you're crying! I can't remember the last time you did that." Harriet laughed, and Louisa quickly brushed her happy tears away.

"You were always a tease, Harriet. But it's so good to see you again at last!"

A porter asked for directions regarding Harriet's luggage, and Louisa sent him to the carriage with it. Harriet slipped her arm through Louisa's, and they walked from the congested platform through the bustling station and out to the street together, comparing notes and laughing at silly things Harriet had experienced on the train.

"If you'd told me how much fun it is to take a train across the country, I would have been out here years ago," Harriet said.

"All I remember from my journey was worry about Charles and how exhausted I was when I got here at last," Louisa said. "The first trip was magical, but I never want to repeat the second." She paused as they got into the carriage. "How is everyone back home? Louise-Caroline? Rebecca and George? Charles? The children?"

"Green with envy is how they are. If Louise-Caroline could have gotten into my trunk she would have come along. Rebecca has decided the Indians aren't going to shoot up every train, and everyone but Charles wished me a good journey."

"Still stubborn. Well, that's his nature." Louisa shook her head. "He misses so much of life by being that way. I feel sorry for him."

"From a distance," Harriet smirked.

"Absolutely," Louisa smiled.

They looked out the window contentedly during the short journey from the station to the house. Harriet was amazed at the activity all around her. After quiet Boston, Denver seemed like an ant mound ready to explode. Louisa tried to see it all through Harriet's eyes—as she'd seen it seven years ago—but found she was so accustomed to Denver's growth that she couldn't do it.

"I want you to relax today and just enjoy being here," Louisa said. "I discovered that a full day of rest after that journey is most beneficial. Then we'll begin our adventures."

"Couldn't we begin them right now?" Harriet urged. "I want to see everything, do everything, meet everyone."

Louisa lay a hand on her arm. "Slow down. We'll do all that and more. You're here for a month unless you extend your stay. We have time, and you are more tired than you think."

After entering the house and meeting the staff, Harriet went to her room, following the trail of her luggage up the stairs. She swept off her hat, spun with delight in the sunlit room, and fell backward on the soft bed.

In less than a minute, she was sound asleep.

Downstairs, Louisa listened to the cessation of sound from above and smiled to herself.

~   ~   ~

"You said you want to see absolutely everything, so I'm going to take you at your word," Louisa said the following day at breakfast. "I don't want to wear you out, but we have a full week of activities to start your visit. Then we can slow down and return to places you want to see again."

"I'm in your hands," Harriet said, dusting her lips with her napkin and lifting her coffee cup from its saucer. "Where you go, I go. But please, I must see the things you've written about."

Ingrid bustled in from the kitchen carrying a large wicker basket and set it gently at the other end of the dining table. "I've arranged everything, ma'am," she said and departed. Louisa's smile stretched across her face, expanding light wrinkles into canyons of delight.

"We'll start with the most wonderful thing of all—a picnic in the mountains," she said. Harriet's eyes danced, and she quickly drank the rest of her coffee.

"I had hoped we'd do that, but on my first day, it's too good to be true!"

Both women pushed away from the table and went to their rooms to don shawls and hats, check themselves in the mirrors, and hurry back down to the hall. Louisa retrieved the basket, and a knock sounded at the door.

"Morning, Miss Hovey," a rough but kindly man said as he saw them. He quickly moved to relieve her of the burden of the basket. "I can see you are ready to go. We're in good time to enjoy the day." Over his shoulder, Louisa and Harriet could see the carriage and a shy woman looking out of it. Two small heads bounced back and forth from seat to seat inside.

"Harriet, this is Ralph. He has always been my guide to the mountains. The first time I went, I invited him to bring his family, and we had a lovely time, so I asked him to bring them again. I hope that is acceptable to you." She turned to Ralph. "This is my dear friend Miss Davenport. She arrived yesterday, so let's give her the scenic tour."

Harriet clapped her hands and grinned. "Perfect!"

Ralph nodded and led the way to the carriage, where Louisa made introductions. Though Priscilla was inclined to be quiet in the company of the older women, Harriet's chatter quickly brought her out of her shell. Betsy was becoming a beautiful young lady and was thrilled to have new ladies to study for their clothing and manners. Her younger brother busily rolled a wooden toy cart across his mother's lap.

"Miss Hovey said you are a teacher, too?" Priscilla asked, noting the ease Harriet had with Betsy's inquisitive explorations.

"My, yes. I teach little boys like your handsome son. They are nowhere as sweet as Betsy or your well-behaved Franklin, and I do not miss them. Louisa and I taught at the same school before she escaped to your wonderful city."

"Did you really escape?" Betsy asked with eyes wide in wonder.

"It certainly felt like escaping," Louisa told her. "I left at night on a train while only Harriet and one other friend knew I was going away. I didn't want anybody to stop me from moving to Denver."

"I'm glad you came!" said Betsy. "My daddy has been so much more fun since you did. We never got to the mountains so much before."

The women all laughed. "We're truly grateful for your patronage," Priscilla said shyly, lowering her eyes.

"Priscilla," Louisa said gently, "I hope that you see us as friends by now. I can't think of anybody I'd want to go on a picnic with more than you and your family. It's only right that I pay for Ralph's time since he can't earn money in the city all day, and the horse needs to be fed and cared for. Thank you for coming with him and bringing the children. It's a treat for us."

Priscilla seemed more comfortable after that. Franklin nearly fell out of the carriage, pointing at a dog here and a funny man there, and then settled onto his mother's lap to sleep for a while. The women talked and got to know each other. By the time they reached the picnic spot, the holiday mood was in full force.

Harriet stepped down from the carriage and stopped, her hand on her chest. "Oh, Louisa," she breathed. "You write lovely letters, but you did not come close to describing this!" She stepped forward slowly, her eyes roving over the towering cliffs and her ears drinking in the sound of the nearby stream. She didn't even notice when the others spread the blanket on the ground and spread the many items from the basket. They had to call her twice before she turned and came to sit with them.

Ingrid knew these picnics were a particular passion of her mistress, so she packed the basket with everything she knew Louisa enjoyed. There was nothing in the basket that would go uneaten. Special sweets for Betsy and Franklin brightened the eyes of the children, and Ralph dined well on thick meat sandwiches. Priscilla even let down her guard enough to try a little wine.

After the meal, Louisa and Harriet rose and ambled across the meadow to the roaring stream that bordered it. The rapids gave it a force they could feel in their chests, and they had to raise their voices to be heard. They settled on rocks on the bank and gazed mesmerized at the torrent that tumbled down from the mountain peaks above.

"I don't know how you could pull yourself away from here and return to Boston after that first trip, Louisa."

"When I would walk out in the garden after dinner each night, I would lift my eyes to the sky and imagine mountains cloaked in darkness, just out of sight. If I could have flown through the air to anywhere on Earth, this is where I would have touched down," Louisa mused.

"I had no idea. You hid it very well."

Louisa turned to look at her. "Talking about it and pining for it wouldn't have served any purpose, would they? I knew at my core that I would one day live here, so I set about making it happen one step at a time. Finding the funds through Melissa's land transactions, putting together the things I wanted to have here when I arrived, bringing Herbert into the plan. . . ." Her face dimmed.

"You know he loved you, don't you?" Harriet put her hand on Louisa's and squeezed. "He may have started to court you because of the lies Charles told those in the Regimental Club about your non-existent dowry, but when you made him your ally, he also became more than a friend."

"I know. I felt bad leaving him behind, but this was a journey I knew I needed to make on my own. He could never have torn himself from Boston for me—and if he did, he would have regretted it eventually."

"When he died," Harriet looked swiftly at Louisa, "he left a note for you. I didn't want to mail it, so I brought it with me. This seems the perfect place to give it to you."

Louisa's surprise was evident. She reached slowly for the small folded paper Harriet had extracted from her dress pocket.

September 28, 1887, Roxbury

Dearest Louisa,

I know I am dying. The doctors make encouraging sounds, but it is all just trumpets at night. They are too weak to tell me, but I know. I think of you as I lie here, and I want to thank you for my "trip" to Colorado. Your spirit, your stories, and your adventure

97

became my own in a very special way. Be free, be well, and be happy, my dear.

Love, Herbert

Harriet rose and wandered along the bank, stooping to play throw-the-stick-in-the-river with Franklin. The sun glinted off the tops of the rapids and made sparkling rainbows as the water leaped over rocks and cascaded ever downward toward the city. Priscilla called Betsy to gather wildflowers with her.

Louisa rose and joined Harriet at the water's edge when she could. Harriet hugged her and looked into her face to judge her mood.

"He was a special man," she said. "But you've no reason to feel guilty about using him as you did. He agreed most heartily to participate."

"I know," Louisa sighed. "Thank you for bringing me the note. I felt like there was still something dangling in our relationship until I read it." She straightened and shaded her eyes from the sun. "I will do what he said—be free, be well, and be happy. It is the best tribute I can give him."

CHAPTER 15

1888, Denver

A few days after their picnic, Louisa and Harriet again lingered over breakfast to plan their day. The scent of pine logs drifted through the open windows, and the sounds of wagons transporting them from building sites to sawmills made a pleasant background.

"What shall we do today?" Harriet asked, folding her napkin and placing her fork precisely across her plate.

"Today we are going shopping."

"You haven't shown me the shops yet, so that will be fun," Harriet said.

"We're not going to the shops. We're going shopping for land."

Harriet squealed. "Really? Honestly? Oh, how exciting!"

"Melissa has found something she wants me to see, which will finally give the two of you a chance to meet. She is most eager to get to know you. I think the two of you will get on very well."

"At last! I was afraid you were keeping her from me," Harriet laughed.

"She is very busy as a purchasing agent and handling her land. This is the first opportunity we've had since you arrived, and it will give you a look at how we buy and sell properties. I admit I'm intrigued to see what she is so avid about. Her note last night was very brief," Louisa said, pushing back her chair. "Let's get ready, and I'll have Ingrid call up the carriage.

Within the half-hour, they were rumbling across Denver in the direction of the place Melissa said she'd meet them. They paused for several minutes to watch the activity at Capitol Hill, where construction had at long last begun.

The size of the project and the number of men was impressive. The materials they were using were arranged around the site, and it was clear it would be a building of which the whole state could be proud. However, they could tell it would be years before the workers completed the job.

Their carriage pulled up behind Melissa's, and she appeared outside their window.

"You're here! I was afraid I'd have to beat people off with a stick if you didn't arrive and make a decision with me," she said.

Catching a glimpse of Harriet, she opened the door and assisted her down, embracing her warmly. "Harriet! Oh, my. It's good to meet you in person at last!"

Harriet rocked back a bit in the face of Melissa's enthusiasm. Louisa was well accustomed to it. She patted Melissa's shoulder and smiled.

"Now Melissa, slow down. You'll wear Harriet out." Melissa looked only slightly abashed.

"When you see what I've got, you'll be just as keen." She turned and began to walk across the land. They followed her eagerly.

"Do you know what you're standing on?" Melissa asked, turning and holding out her arms to encompass the area around her.

Louisa studied the parcel and turned around to see what surrounded it. "Isn't this Brown's land? I heard he has held some back."

"The part he's held back. . . *until today*," Melissa said. "I got word last night that he's opening it up for purchase and development. This is the opportunity we've been waiting for, Louisa."

Harriet watched the two women and gazed at the open ground. Not a tree was in sight. The flat plain looked barren and uninteresting, like much of what she'd crossed on the train from Boston. She frowned and tried to see what they were seeing but was baffled.

"Hmm." Louisa looked around again. "How much of it?"

"The equivalent of 45 lots," Melissa crowed. "What could we do with that!"

Louisa was astonished. "We've never bought anything so big before. Can we afford it?"

"He wants $2500. It's going to be a stretch, no question about it. But Louisa," Melissa gripped her friend's arm in a steely clasp, "In a year, maybe less, this could be the complete making of both of us. We have to ride out the lack of cash for a bit."

Harriet could stand it no longer. "Wait, what is so special about this piece of dry ground that you'd put so much money on it?"

They both turned to her, and she realized they'd forgotten she was even there. They looked at each other sheepishly, then began to speak simultaneously.

"The first thing--" Melissa said.

"You have to understand--" Louisa said.

Both of them laughed. Melissa took a step back. "Let's see how much you've learned, Louisa. You tell her why it's important for us."

Louisa took a breath and ordered her thoughts. Then she turned to Harriet.

"The most important thing about any land is where it is. That's even more important than whether it has trees, a stream, or anything else." She looked to see if Harriet was following her. Her friend nodded.

"Do you remember the construction at the Capitol we passed?"

Harriet nodded again. "This parcel is just far enough away from that to make for quiet home sites. But it is also close enough that people who do business at the Capitol will want to live here. That makes it a prime place."

"All right. What else?" Harriet was intrigued.

Louisa turned and gestured. "It's flat. There are no trees on it. No bog or stream is running through it that can flood in the spring. That means there is a lot less for buyers to do before they build. So we can charge a little extra for each lot because it will still be cheaper than a place they must adjust first."

"How much would you get for it?" Harriet's stance conveyed her excitement.

"That depends," Louisa said, looking at Melissa. "We could sell it off as 45 individual lots. What's the going rate for a lot right now?"

"In this area, $100," Melissa said. "Or. . ."

"Yes, I know." Louisa turned back to Harriet. "So if we did that, we could sell it for $4500. Or, we could break it into bigger lots for people who want to build bigger homes. We'd have fewer lots, but those folks expect to pay more for their land." She again looked to Melissa. "Do you think $500 each?" Melissa nodded. "So that would make $7500."

Harriet whistled. "So you spend $2500 and make either $4500 or even $7500? What's even to consider?"

Both Louisa and Melissa laughed. Melissa took over the conversation.

"There's a reason why they call it land speculation, my dear," she said. "These are the going rates. But numbers fluctuate all the time. Our values can drop quickly if someone opens up more land—or even if Mr. Brown opens up more land. More pieces mean more competition."

"But you'd make at least what you spent, right?" Harriet puzzled.

"We would certainly hope so," Louisa smiled. "But we could make just about what we spent and tie up our money for a year or even more to do it. That's the gamble."

"Oh, my," Harriet sighed and rubbed her forehead. "I begin to see both the fun and the danger in what you two are doing."

They all stood silently gazing at the open fields, thinking. But when another carriage drew up, Melissa quickly turned to Louisa again.

"I say we do it. What do you think? We have to act fast or lose it."

Louisa's eyes grazed the waving grasses and wildflowers before she turned to Melissa. "Yes. Let's do it." Harriet's eyes grew large, and she gulped.

Looking at the men leaving the carriage, Melissa whispered, "Let me handle this. Just go quietly to your carriage."

As they returned to the rough road where they'd parked and passed the men, she said to Louisa and Harriet, "Well, I am going to have to think about it. We don't have the funds right now. Let's sleep on it and come look at it again next week."

Both men's eyes glinted as they exchanged looks and passed the women. When they were out of earshot, Melissa murmured to Louisa, "See you at the Land Office as fast as you can. Mr. Brown said he'd be there all day."

~ ~ ~

Harriet sat in the garden of Louisa's home and watched bees buzzing over the profusion of flowers that bordered it and hugged the walkway. She thought about Louisa. Her friend had changed and yet not changed in the years since they'd last seen each other.

Louisa had always been a thinker and a doer. The fact that she'd come West at all showed that. When her friend had moved here over her family's protest, it confirmed how strong-willed Louisa could be. But watching her in action last week as she and Melissa first examined the land and then raced to the Land Office to meet Mr. Brown and negotiate its purchase had been breathtaking.

They'd arrived and found him talking with several men at a table in the corner of the office. However, he rose when Melissa approached, having long done business with her. His respect for and wariness of her business sense was evident.

After introducing Miss Hovey and Miss Davenport, Melissa got down to business. Initially offering a good bit less than the $2500 asking price, she and Brown gradually danced back and forth until Louisa and Melissa spent $2550 for the parcel. Melissa explained afterward that she was ready to go higher and could have driven a hard bargain to go lower, but by giving Brown a bit over what he initially asked, he felt like he'd won. She and Louisa had been the big winners, however.

"Is there anything she can't do?" Harriet mused aloud. She jumped when Louisa's voice replied from behind her. "Who and what?" she asked.

"You and all the things you have accomplished. You are a wonder, Louisa."

Louisa sat in another of the lawn chairs and smiled softly. "I was a teacher; it taught me how to recognize other teachers, like Melissa, and to latch on to them when I find them. Half of intelligence is knowing where to find the information you need."

Harriet's delighted laugh rang through the sunny garden. "I have told my students the same thing to no avail for years." Louisa laughed as well.

A shadow fell over them both, and a softly accented baritone voice drew their quick attention.

"There is nothing so beautiful as lovely ladies laughing in a garden!"

They both stood and turned quickly to see an average-height man with handsome features, dark brown hair, and lively brown eyes standing nearby. He bowed in an old-world manner, and his smile flashed broad and white.

"Please do not let me disturb you. I was making a delivery and could not help but see the picture of you both in the sun in your lovely dresses that look like blossoms. Then you laughed, and it rang in my soul."

"My goodness," Harriet said, looking at Louisa.

"You must be Ernest," Louisa said, narrowing her eyes. "Ingrid has told me you have the silver tongue of the Old Country, though you don't come from Ireland, I can tell."

Ernest bowed slightly again. "No, my family is from lovely France," his accent seemed to smooth the words in a buttery way. "Were I not the son of the fourth son of a duke, I would still be there. Alas, I have had to make my way in the world but have found much wonder and joy in this land of Colorado."

Harriet grinned broadly, enjoying the charm that seemed to ooze from Ernest's pores. Louisa snorted.

"And what have you brought us today, Ernest?" she asked, trying to direct him back to his business.

"Ah, Miss Hovey," he pronounced it *Ho-vee*, "much that is delectable to grace your table! Oysters from the East, greens from the West, tender beef from the North, and the sweetest possible sugarcane from the South."

With another shake of her head, Louisa acknowledged that he had a way with words. "All right then, be on your way and make Ingrid happy with one of your visits. But don't try to steal her from me," she warned. "She's too good for the slippery likes of you."

Placing a graceful hand over his heart and with an expression of genuine hurt, Ernest once again bowed. Then, with a smile to Harriet and a modified salute to Louisa, he sauntered back to the kitchen door and his delivery cart.

"Oh, Louisa, keep an eye on that one," Harriet whispered, watching him go.

CHAPTER 16

Spring 1889, Denver

Dear Harriet,

Your last letter made me feel old. Imagine a precocious little boy like Guy Holliday preparing to graduate from Harvard! I still picture him in short pants and with that insolent grin. He had the intelligence to go far—I just wasn't sure he'd apply himself properly. I stand corrected.

Each day when I rise and look out my windows, I remember your delight in the mountains and how you fell in love with them during your visit last summer, just as I have. I can no longer imagine a skyline without them. The thought of Boston, so closed in and tight-knit, is enough to make me run outside and take deep breaths of mountain air, even if it's tinged with the scent of ore smelting and wood shavings.

Melissa has returned from another of her lengthy trips. This time, she went south to Mexico and even into Guatemala. Amazing!

She brought me some wonderful wall hangings made from bird feathers. She does love to travel. She is so good at land transactions because they feed her other addiction to wandering the world. I'm glad she always comes home. She has told some fabulous tales and almost convinced me that I should also try traveling. Almost.

I know you remember when we looked at some land, and Melissa and I bought it. We've held it against the day when buyers would bring us the right price. That day has arrived.

Much to my astonishment, and thanks to Melissa's astute thinking, we've divided up that large parcel and the pieces are selling briskly. It helps that one of the first buyers is a prominent citizen of Denver with plans to build a very large home on four adjacent lots. The herd has followed, and we stand to make many times what we invested!

So, the kernel of a dream of seeing the world is not far-fetched, after all.

Love,
Louisa

Louisa reviewed her household ledgers again and sat back with a sigh of satisfaction. She received pay for teaching in Boston but never really had money to spare. Over their objections, she contributed to Rebecca and George's expenses and helped run the household to give Rebecca a break. Then, she put aside what she could. Now, the numbers in the account were larger than she had ever seen on paper—at least her paper.

She turned to the map on her wall. Melissa had given it to her as a birthday gift with money as an incentive to plan a trip. She enthused long and poetically over the fascinating things Louisa might experience abroad. Judging by the souvenirs Melissa returned with, the stories were true.

What would it be like to pack a trunk, buy a ticket, plan a route, and just. . . go? She looked around her at the comfortable room she used as her study. She leased her house. She could pay the rent in advance while she was away. Or if she planned to be gone an extended period, store everything and rent a new home later.

Louisa found herself jotting notes to herself on a pad of paper. What to do about Ingrid and other household staff? When was a good time to travel? What would she need to take with her? How did one go about purchasing all the necessary tickets and documents? It all began to whirl in her mind and overwhelm her orderly planning.

Of course, she needed to answer the most crucial question first: *Where would she like to go?*

It was a relief when Ingrid knocked softly on the door and announced Melissa, who swept into the room with her usual energy and confidence. Louisa rose and embraced her.

"I'm so glad to see you! I'm giving myself a headache, and it's all your fault," Louisa laughed.

Melissa cocked an eyebrow and narrowed her eyes. "What in the world are you up to?"

Louisa walked to the map and put her palm on it. "What in the world—exactly," she said. "I was sitting here daydreaming about taking a trip. I started making lists of things to do and then realized I had no idea where I wanted to go. That's when the headache started."

Melissa laughed. "That's the easy part! Since you are new to this, there is only one possible answer. Go around the world."

Louisa gasped and turned back to the map. "Around the—?" Her eyes grew wide. "You mean the whole world?"

"It's a grand idea. It will give you a taste of many different places during one trip, and you'll know where you want to return to on subsequent trips to enjoy more time."

"Subsequent trips!" Louisa squeaked. "I just wanted to go somewhere, not make this a lifetime habit."

"And why not? People do, you know. I certainly do. There is something so interesting about listening to different languages, tasting foods you've never heard of, and trying things you'll never find here—like riding a llama or canoeing on the Amazon. And then you come back here and fall in love with Denver all over again until the travel bug bites."

A frown formed on Louisa's broad brow. "Other languages. I hadn't thought about that. I don't speak any other languages. This is getting complicated."

With a firm hand on Louisa's arm, Melissa looked her in the eyes. "It's not complicated. You need the right help. You need to hire a concierge."

"What? Like at the hotel?"

"No, someone who will handle all the details and leave you free to enjoy. He buys the tickets, arranges the tours, keeps track of your luggage—which will increase as you go—and steps in when things inevitably go wrong. He's indispensable."

"And you do this for all your trips? Who do you use?"

"Oh, I use different people every time to have the best one for where I'm going. However, a trip around the world requires someone committed to the journey and flexible enough to handle the details. Also, you want someone who will be fun to have along. Nothing is worse than dragging a boring person after you for months."

Ingrid returned with a tray of coffee and cakes, deposited it on the side table, and left. Louisa and Melissa made up their coffees and plates and moved back to the map.

"I suggest you do this in the most interesting way. Why not go West to East? Most Americans go the other way. That would add to the fun. Start on the West Coast and head for Japan. That's my recommendation. Then, we went to India, sailed through the Suez Canal, and finished in Europe for a Grand Tour. Come back by way of Boston so you can impress your relations there. Then get yourself back to Denver and tell me all about it."

"Gracious!" Louisa put her hand to her heart. "No, that's too much. I want to try traveling, not make it my whole life. I was thinking maybe Europe. . . ."

"Whether you take on the world or just get your feet wet, you must go. That's settled. But first, get your man of business lined up. It's vital."

They sipped coffee and savored Ingrid's wonderful lemon cake as they considered the problem. Melissa raised and dismissed one name after another, each for different reasons.

"Mr. Fulsom is already in Europe for the foreseeable future with Mrs. Scott and her daughters. Mr. Smithson. . . no, he only does short trips now. What about. . . ? Oh, I forgot. He's one of the most inflexible people I know. I want you to be able to have adventures, not keep to a timetable."

For her part, Louisa was surprised that so many people in Denver specialized in such travel arrangements. She sneaked another piece of cake while Melissa mused and stirred more cream into a fresh cup of coffee.

"Well, he's out there somewhere. We have to find him. I'll ask around." Melissa finished her coffee and decisively set down her cup and saucer. "I just stopped in to see how you are and bask in our success's glow. I'm so glad you are taking my advice to heart."

"I always do, Melissa."

They rose and embraced, and suddenly, the room felt bereft because the light and force that was Melissa had rushed off to yet another project.

~   ~   ~

In Louisa's garden, summer was threatening to give way to the browns of autumn, and she enjoyed walking in the yard in the late afternoons to note the changes. Birds were restless as though preparing to head south. Greens were shading toward brown, though the fall flowers were still not blooming.

She pondered the problem of finding a man of business to accompany her on her trip for what felt like the fiftieth time. The fact that she now considered it *her trip* was not lost on her. Considering the immensity of the project, she'd gone from a quaint suggestion to actual planning rather quickly.

Rich laughter drew her attention to the kitchen door, where Ingrid's blush told her who the chuckle came from. She was about to turn away when a thought occurred to her, and she walked with purpose around the hedge and into the driveway.

Her sudden appearance caused Ingrid to straighten and prepare to return to the kitchen but only brought a bigger smile to Ernest's face.

"Ah, the divine Miss Ho-vee! I am so delighted to see you on this lovely afternoon." He made his three-second shallow bow, straightened, and looked into her eyes. Indeed, he was like no grocery delivery man she'd ever heard of. But that was what inspired her at that moment.

"Ernest, Mister—by the way, what is your last name? I never asked."

"Sasseville, my lady. Ernest Max Sasseville at your service."

Again, the bow. It could have been annoying, but he did it with such dignity and grace that she rather enjoyed it.

"Mr. Sasseville, I suspect you are friendly with people in many of the finer homes where you deliver goods, are you not?"

He looked abashed. "I'm sorry, madam. Have I offended in some way?" He glanced at Ingrid's retreating form and then back at Louisa.

She shook her head. "Not at all. I need a particular type of service, and I have a feeling you can either find me the person I need or you can inquire at the homes you visit."

"Ah, *mais oui*! I can procure for you anything you need—from parsnips to people! I would consider it an honor. Just tell me what you need, kind lady."

"I am planning to take a trip abroad, and I want to find a man of business to handle the details for me and serve as my escort. My friend Miss Hotchkiss has been unable to locate someone who can go with me despite months of trying. Would you be willing to ask around and find out who has served other people in this way and bring me some names?"

"When would you be traveling, Miss Ho-vee? And to where? That will have a bearing on the person I recommend."

111

"That's a bit complicated. I plan to start in Europe, but it may be a lengthy trip, and I need someone I could get along with well.

"One who speaks languages, who has traveled before. Someone who understands foreign customs and has the flexibility to deal with the problems that might arise, who can suggest destinations *en route*, no?"

Louisa took a deep breath of relief. "Yes, that is exactly right. Do you think you can find someone?"

"But of course! I know of just the person for you. I only have to check his availability. When do you plan to begin this odyssey of delight?"

"I would like to be gone for the winter, so in the late autumn. I don't know how long it will take.

"Perfect! I shall return tomorrow with the man!"

CHAPTER 17

Late Summer 1889, Denver

It rained the next day, and Louisa stood at her study window, watching the droplets slide down the panes. She'd been restless all day, and the thunder and downpour earlier in the day had shaken the walls of the house and made her uneasy.

"It's just rain," she told herself. "It will pass." Still, in her mind, she pictured the water rushing through the ordinarily dry rivers that divided the city and wondered what damage would be done. It was one reason she'd agreed with Melissa's advice that they stick to land, not buildings. Land endured.

Ingrid had already lit the lamps in the room to push back the gloom, and a fire burned in the fireplace. Louisa moved to stand before the blaze and enjoyed watching the colors of the flames slide over each other in endless motion. When a knock sounded on the door, she turned.

"Come in."

"Ah, my dear Miss Ho-vee! What a day this is! What water comes from the skies, and it seems to have nowhere to go. Were I a duck, I would be very happy, but as it is, I am much better pleased to be in this cozy room with you."

Louisa smiled wryly. "Mr. Sasseville. I thought perhaps you would put off your visit until tomorrow so that you would not have to get out in this storm." She looked him up and down. He wore an impeccable suit of dark fabric, and his shoes shoned. How had he come through the rain so well?

"If the need were not urgent I do not think I would have attempted it," he said with his signature bow. "But I knew you were most anxious to finalize your travel details, and so I have brought to you the man you require."

Louisa shifted her gaze to the hall behind him. It was empty. "Where is he, then?"

Ernest squared his shoulders and stepped forward one pace. "It is I."

"It is me," she corrected without thought. He looked puzzled.

Then she startled. "You mean you have brought me yourself to be my man of business?"

"Absolutely, madam. I could entrust your safety and your satisfaction to no one else."

"Mr. Sasseville," she began gently, "I need someone who has seen the world and can show it to me. It is true that you have been very helpful in keeping this household supplied with what we need, but this is a completely different situation."

"Do you think I am a grocery delivery man from my birth?" he asked in amazement. "Did I not tell you of my noble lineage in la belle France? Do I not speak the tongues of Europe more easily than English? No, madam, I am the man for you."

"How's your Hungarian?" she asked, thinking to put him off.

"How is yours?" He laughed. "Oh, madam, no one knows every language in the world. That is what interpreters are for. What is needed is a person who knows how to procure such help in every country along your route."

He was right. She was intrigued. She again looked him over. He was strong, that was clear. He knew how to dress—he'd proved that by arriving in a suit. Somehow, he'd come through the storm and arrived in her study in refined style. But was it enough?

"Why would you want to come with me? What about your family? I plan to be away for some time. What about your job?"

"Pffff!" he snorted. "My job is whatever gives me the freedom to do what I like. I can put it down and pick up another one later. Do not concern yourself with that. I am, how you say, free as the bird."

"I don't even know how to negotiate an agreement with someone for this service. I was counting on the man of business to tell me his terms. I'm confused."

"Put your mind at rest, Miss Ho-vee. I would be honored to accompany, guide, and protect you all the way around the world if need be. You do not have to pay me; just pay my way."

Louisa's eyebrows rose. "Surely you want to be paid. Otherwise, you will return here none the better for your service to me."

"To see many places I have read about, to have adventures, and to see your face light up with delight as I introduce you to it all. . . these are my pay. And I will not come back none the better, as you say. I will come back much better for the experience. Who knows, I could begin a whole new career."

Louisa moved to a chair and sank into it. It was too much and too sudden. "I need to think about this." She saw the light brighten in his eyes. "I'm not saying I'll take you on," she said, raising one hand, "but I will think about it."

"That is all I could expect, madam. I shall bid you a good day and good thinking."

~   ~   ~

September 10, 1889, Denver

Dear Harriet,

I wish I had your clear head here to advise me. You are so able to see alternate solutions to problems. I may have gotten myself into a situation.

115

As I told you, Melissa recommended securing a man of business to escort me on my trip. I fully understand the need for that. I want to relax, enjoy it all, and not worry about whether my hat box got on the wrong train.

But she's been unable to find me someone who fits the bill despite looking for months and checking with all her friends. Many of them are currently traveling and have taken up all the usual men of business who are willing to go on long journeys. However, I have found someone that I am considering.

You will no doubt be shocked, Harriet. It's Ernest Sasseville. Yes, the delivery man.

Now, before you grab your pen and paper to send me a letter of rebuke, think about it. He says he has international experience. At the very least, he speaks French. He says he speaks German and Italian, as well. I have no way to verify that as I don't speak a word of anything but English.

The fact that he's charming is a bonus. The fact that he is nearly young enough to be my son is a protection. His enthusiasm for the project is high, and he only asks me to pay his way. He may parlay this experience into providing similar services to other women once we return. I think he'd be good at it. Actually, he'd be good at anything to which he turned his hand.

When I consider that I could be giving him a leg up to a new career, I almost convince myself to hire him. But what do you think? Have I reached my dotage and lost perspective? I'll only be 50 next year. However, I will be 50! If I am going to do this, I should do it while I am young enough to indulge in it.

Do send me your thoughts,
Louisa

~   ~   ~

September 16, 1889, Boston

Dear Louisa:

All right, my jaw has finally closed again after reading your letter. My initial reaction was to remind you of what I said when I met the very charming Ernest when I visited you: Watch out for that one. My experience with charming men is limited but has usually been of the negative—though stimulating—variety.

That was my first thought, but after further reflection, I can also see your logic. When I picture someone described as a "man of business," all I can see is an old stick of a man who says "no" to ice cream before dinner. The thought of dragging such a being around the world to ease one's way and prevent gossip is unbearable.

Ernest, on the other hand. . . . He'd be fun, wouldn't he?

Could he stay the course and stay with you the whole trip? Or would he find some fetching woman in Barcelona, Florence, or Paris and abandon you? Does he have ulterior motives in mind? Is he after your money?

Your decision must depend on how much you trust him and how much leeway you're willing to give him. Indeed, he will make some mistakes during a long trip like that. How much can you tolerate? In short, do you grab the amusing man and go, or wait for an old stick?

I know you'll choose well, if unexpectedly. You always do.

Harriet

~ ~ ~

Things to do before leaving Denver

- Get proper trunk and luggage for extended use
- Assemble clothing for many climates and situations
- Visit with friends for possible destinations and advice
- Ask for guidebooks they may have found helpful
- Find a temporary situation for Ingrid and other staff
- Arrange for furniture to be stored
- Apply for passport
- Organize the necessary paperwork to take
- Notify all services of date to stop deliveries
- Notify family of intention to travel

She chewed the end of her pen for a moment as she thought and then added one last item.

- Hire Ernest Sasseville

CHAPTER 18

October 1889, Boston

For the first time in more than seven years, Louisa stood in the entry hall of her half-sister's home, with Rebecca directing the footman to carry her luggage to her old room and George smiling a warm welcome. As she gazed around her, she saw what she had expected—absolutely nothing had changed.

"We're so glad to have you home, even if you say it is temporary," George said with a wink.

"It seemed the most sensible way since I needed to apply for my passport. It will arrive here sooner than it would have in Denver. I canceled my lease there. I currently have no address and appreciate you letting me use yours."

Rebecca moved in for another hug. "I don't care why you're home. I'm just so happy you are here." Her squeeze reminded Louisa of one of the few things she'd missed.

"Of course, I will help you with the house as before. I don't want to be a burden."

"Family is never a burden!" Rebecca exclaimed. A shadow fell briefly over her lovely face. Louisa knew it was because the two of them had lived alone in this house all their married life except when

George's mother lived with them. Children had never come, and Rebecca ached to have people around her to love.

"It's kind of you to say, Rebecca. I'm not sure Charles will share your generous spirit. How is he? How are Louise-Caroline and the children?"

"They are scarcely children anymore. Edith is 21, and Rebecca is 18. Carl is 16 and very independent."

"And I'm happy to say he shows a certain literary bent," George said with pride. His efforts in publishing kept him aware of anyone around him who liked to write, and finding such a person in his extended family was a double delight.

"But we've loads of time to catch up," Rebecca said, guiding her to the foot of the broad stairs. "You go freshen up from your travels and then we can talk all evening."

In truth, Louisa was relieved to escape to her small, quiet room. On the trip east, she'd thought of little else except the reception she might receive at home. Letters reassuring her of a place with them again did not ease her mind, but George's and Rebecca's greeting had been wonderful.

There was still the matter of Charles. . .

~   ~   ~

"So tell me everything!" Harriet cried when Louisa met her at their old favorite tea room. "I want all the details. When do you leave? How are you getting along with Ernest? How does your family like him? How long will you be gone?"

Louisa waved a hand to stem the flow of questions. "Harriet, do you never take a breath?"

"Oh, Louisa, there's no time to breathe around you. You're always on the move and doing something interesting." They gave the waiter their favorite order for tea, sandwiches, and cakes and spent a moment settling into the wicker chairs more comfortably.

"I must say you're looking well, Louisa. Denver has agreed with you. How is Melissa?"

Louisa thought for a moment. "Moving to Denver was the best thing I've ever done, not because of the town itself but because of what it represents for me. It meant breaking out of the lifelong rut I was in. It meant taking a chance, diving into something without complete assurance it would work out. I think it was the making of me." She stirred cream into her tea. "Melissa sends her warm greetings. She's ecstatic that I will finally follow her travel suggestion."

Harriet nodded. "When you first said you were moving to Denver, I did think you were a bit mad, but I was also excited for you. Then, when I went out and saw you there last year, I could tell it fit you just perfectly. It's such a jumped-up town! So much energy. And it is so beautiful once you escape the noise and the bustle. I felt tempted to pull up stakes and join you."

Louisa laughed. "Oh, that would have turned Denver on its ear! You, me, and Melissa in tandem. I'm not sure society would ever recover." Harriet joined in the laughter, ate a cake, and wiped her mouth.

"And Ernest? Is he as outrageously charming and handsome as I remember? What does your family think of him?"

Louisa lowered her head and her voice. "They haven't met him and I'm trying to keep it that way. As far as they know, I've hired a boring old man of business to guide me through Europe. I confess I had second thoughts about the whole thing when I realized how they'd react to him."

"Then where is he? Still in Denver?"

"No. He went on to Rochester. He has relatives there, apparently, and he's staying there to work on our travel plans and documents. I'm very glad he's not here. I'm meeting Charles and his family at dinner later this week. Can you imagine Ernest and Charles in the same room?"

Harriet's eyes twinkled. "I think it would be a real test of his charm!"

"Charles does not succumb to charm. He'd probably pull his sword off the mantle and thrash Ernest with the flat of it for trying." They both laughed at the mental image.

"Maybe you're right. But they'll have to meet him before you go, right?"

"Not if I can help it. I told them I'd meet him at the dock when I left for my trip. If I'm fortunate, none of the family will make the trip to see me off."

"Well, I certainly will. I need to assure myself he's got your arrangements well in hand. And nothing else!"

~   ~   ~

October 25, 1889, Rochester, NY

My Dear Miss Hovey:

I trust that you are having an enjoyable time renewing acquaintances with your family after so many years. I have also been getting to know my family once more. There have been many new Sassevilles for me to meet since I was last here!

I received my passport document today. I trust you have also received yours since I submitted them at the same time. This is excellent news since it means I can now book passage for us across the Atlantic. I believe that we should be able to travel within a few short weeks. I will supply the exact details when I have them.

Prepare yourself for a magnificent time of exploration, discovery, and delight! We shall begin in London and then make a complete circuit of the Continent, lingering in any destination you find attractive. I look forward to seeing the light of joy rise in your eyes!

Your Servant,
Ernest Max Sasseville

Louisa folded the letter and placed it in her correspondence box. Having been away from Ernest for a few weeks had dulled her memory of his overwhelming enthusiasm. It fairly rose off the page and she found herself smiling.

She had not smiled when completing the passport application process. First, she'd had to submit to the eagle-eyed view of the passport clerk while he described her on the form.

Age: 49 Years	Mouth: Ordinary
Stature: 5 feet 8 ½ inches	Chin: Round
Forehead: High and full	Hair: Grey
Eyes: Blue	Complexion: Fair
Nose: Small	Face: Full

Saying she had a high and full forehead was fine, but a *full face* made her feel ugly. At least they had not weighed her!

She listed her sister's address as hers and called herself a Housekeeper for the sake of the form. She wondered what Ernest had written there.

She was stumped when the clerk asked when she would return to the country. Finally, she just said, "Within the coming year." It was a sobering moment. She would be away for a whole year! With Ernest! What if he drove her to distraction? What if she were bored or ran out of energy for the project? Would he be unbearably disappointed if she did come home within the coming year and not stay the whole time?

The crisp paper of her large passport, with its official seal, thrilled her. She wondered how worn and stained it would be by the time she again saw Boston. With another sigh, she put all her travel worries away and began to prepare for the family dinner at Charles' and Louise-Caroline's home.

CHAPTER 19

October 25, 1889, Boston

"Louisa." His voice sounded like ice being chipped. She had always considered her brother Charles tall, but he seemed to have added an inch to his stature with the ramrod posture of his back. Even his greeting didn't bend him as his nose twitched and his mustache ruffled over his bottom lip.

Louise-Caroline quickly glanced at her husband, stepped around him, and embraced her sister-in-law with a soft cry. "My dear, it has been so long! Welcome home." Her daughters Edith and Rebecca stood behind her, gloved hands clasped at their waists. They seemed to waver as if caught in the conflicting currents of their parents' emotions. Carl looked her over and stepped forward, his hand extended.

"Aunt Louisa. Welcome."

She smiled at his formal greeting, which was far beyond his sixteen years in its gravity. "Thank you all," she said, her eyes traveling the group. She heard a quiet exhale behind her and realized her sister Rebecca had been holding her breath. George moved to Charles, and they shook hands.

"Sorry we've kept her to ourselves all week, but we thought she needed to rest up a bit after her journey." Rebecca moved up beside him and hugged her brother, Louise-Caroline, and the young people in turn.

So that's what it feels like when ice melts. Well, when it begins to crack, just the slightest bit, anyway.

The evening took on the ageless tempo of Hovey family dinners, established by their father and carried on by Charles ever since. There were drinks in the drawing room. Elegance sparkled in each piece of silver and shimmering candle at the table. The men remained to smoke and drink brandy, Carl self-consciously delighted about being included in the group. The women returned to the drawing room and the fire, to listen to Edith play piano.

Talk at the dinner table had been almost entirely among the men, with the women speaking softly to each other occasionally. Louisa marveled at the entire progression. How had she ever thought this was enough? How had she lasted here so long?

She pictured picnics in the mountains, days walking plots of land with Melissa and haggling over prices with buyers and sellers, great carts of ore and timber rumbling into the city, the cry of drovers urging on their mules. A great wave of homesickness for Denver swept over her.

A rising tide of excitement about her upcoming exploits enabled Louisa to brush the feeling aside. Europe. With Ernest to amuse and guide her, the days would blend into each other as she explored museums, attended concerts, sat in the Spanish sunshine, and listened to the water lap against the buildings in Venice.

Her thoughts must have tinged her face, for her sister leaned toward her on the settee where they sat in the drawing room, and she said, "Tell Louise-Caroline why you've come home, my dear."

She had lost touch with Louise-Caroline over the years because of her brother Charles' objections to their letters. Though Louise-Caroline was spirited enough to go against him if she chose, she also knew the value of peace and tranquility in the house. Her avid expression told Louisa nothing had changed since the days of her escape to Denver.

"I am going to travel, and I plan to be away for at least a year," she said, hearing the women gasp. There is so much I wish to see— London, Paris, and Italy, of course, but perhaps other places as well —even the Middle East. I have the time, and I have the means. My friends bring back such wonderful stories of their trips. Now I can be the one to have interesting things to say."

"You've always been that," Louise-Caroline said. "Even when you were teaching school, you couldn't stop yourself from telling us what you were teaching them and what you were learning alongside them. But a whole year? How will you do it?"

"I was renting my home in Denver and have let it go. The city is booming, and I will have no trouble finding a new one when I return. And I have hired a man of business to escort my luggage and handle my arrangements." Louisa took a sip of her coffee to hide the small smile this fact brought to her face.

"That's the first sensible thing you have ever done," Charles said from the doorway as the men joined the ladies again. They all turned. "It's foolish and dangerous for a woman to wander the world alone. You would only get into trouble without anyone to help you." He sniffed. Obviously, he would not come to her rescue, no matter the circumstances.

"I intend to enjoy my trip," Louisa said, setting her coffee cup on its delicate saucer and placing both on the table next to her. I don't want to worry about timetables, luggage, tickets, and finding interpreters. My friends in Denver who travel regularly suggested a concierge, and I agreed."

"But who is this man? What company does he work for? What is his family background?" Rebecca's brow furrowed. This was the first she'd heard of a companion.

I will ask in the City," Charles said. "I will direct you to the right person for this chore."

Louisa's back stiffened. "I have already engaged my escort, and I am content. I hired him in Denver. He is in Rochester at this moment finalizing our arrangements."

"When will we meet him?" Louise-Caroline offered her more coffee, and she accepted.

"You won't. We will meet at the ship before we sail."

There was a profound silence; Carl's nervous cracking of his knuckles made his mother jump. Charles posed by the fireplace. Abruptly, he put his cup down with a startling rattle.

"Oh, Louisa! Once again, you will leap before you look. Again, you will put yourself in a position to be a laughingstock of the whole city. Why can't you just behave?"

She shook her head as she gazed at him. "Charles, what is it that offends you about me? I have never involved you in my decisions and never come crying to you if something goes wrong. I make my choices, and I stick by them."

He rounded on her. "That's just the point! Women need men to look after them, guide them, and make decisions for them. Why, without that, the world would run off the rails!"

All the tension suddenly drained out of Louisa. She threw back her head and laughed. Charles' jaw dropped. The eyes of the other women grew large.

"I have been such a failure, haven't I? I taught school—and did it well—for many years. Then, I decided to move to Denver because it is beautiful, vibrant, and exciting. I made a fortune—I say again, *a fortune*—buying and selling land there. I made friends. I entered society in a major way. And now I am free to travel the whole world if I wish without care, in complete comfort, and at ease."

Louisa chuckled again. "Everyone should be such a failure, Charles."

She rose from her seat and straightened her gown. She nodded to them all. "I think this is enough of a reunion for one evening, don't you? Perhaps we should be heading home."

Rebecca and George scrambled to their feet as well. Louisa approached Charles, who was still standing immobilized by the fireplace.

"Charles, I want you to know that I love you. We are very different people, but we are family. If you were ever in trouble, I would not hesitate to help you. I hope you can come to see me as the sister who is the least like you but is still quite willing to be your friend."

~ ~ ~

October 28, 1898, Rochester

My Dear Miss Hovey – a very hasty note so I can catch the post. We sail from New York on the Augusta Victoria *of the Hamburg America Line at 9:40 a.m. on November 14. Be ready to catch the tide and sail into adventures! – Ernest Max Sasseville*

CHAPTER 20

November 17, 1889
Aboard the Augusta Victoria

The stiff breeze filled Louisa's lungs as she sat in a deck chair, carefully wrapped in a warm blanket Ernest had solicitously brought her. Her pulse seemed to beat with the tempo of the huge engines that drove the massive ship through the waves. It was the first day of their journey when the sun had shown down directly enough to make it possible to bask on deck, and she was content.

She watched passengers as they walked arm-in-arm on the polished boards and recalled her first sight of the *Augusta Victoria* . The shipping line had aptly named it for an empress. Beautiful in all its lines with three massive smokestacks, luxurious in every appointment. Twin screws drove it through the waters. Ernest told her that on its maiden voyage six months previous, the ship had broken all records by reaching England in just seven days.

Louisa loved hotels, and this magnificent ship was a floating one. Beautiful wood, superb dining facilities, and palm-lined reception areas made her feel she'd never left port. The rococo entry hall's massive stairway glowed with lights held by gilded cherubs. Music filled the air each evening, and the dancing had been exhilarating. She could not have picked a more compelling chariot to bear her toward Europe.

Ernest approached, holding the arm of a sturdy-looking young woman in a blue plaid travel outfit. "Here she is," he said. "You must meet each other!"

Puzzled, Louisa rose from her chair. Ernest was forever finding interesting people on board, and thus far, her trip had been one long greeting ceremony. Who was this woman?

"Miss Hovey, I knew you would want to meet this special passenger. May I present Miss Nellie Bly."

Louisa gasped.

"Why, Miss Bly! I've been following your articles in the *New York World* but never expected to meet you on your long journey. Do sit down, won't you?"

Nellie put out her hand and shook Louisa's firmly. The two women sank into adjacent chairs as Ernest beamed.

"It's nice to meet you, Miss Hovey. Mr. Sasseville here was most insistent that I come to see you. I understand you are on your way for an extended trip on the Continent."

"Yes, we are, but your trip is so much more fascinating. Please tell me how it came about. I have read Mr. Verne's book, *Around the World in 80 Days*. But your journey is not fictional."

Nellie laughed. "It very nearly remained all in my head. I read the book, too, and thought it would be interesting to see if I could beat the fictional tour of Phileas Fogg. My goal is to do it in 74 days or less."

"Miss Bly has studied every timetable in the world to optimize the ships, trains, and other modes of travel to complete her journey as expeditiously as possible," Ernest said. "She puts my poor efforts of shepherding you through Europe to shame."

"And you will be reporting your progress along the way?" Louisa asked.

"I can send brief updates via electric wire wherever available, but I plan to write many articles and perhaps even a book when I get home."

"Why do you say it was almost a journey all in your head?"

"I proposed it to Mr. Pulitzer, and he thought it was a wonderful idea—for a *man* to undertake. In fact, he said he would find a man to do it immediately. I was outraged."

Louisa nodded. "Of course you were! It is an attitude I have encountered myself."

"Mr. Sasseville has told me some of your story, Miss Hovey. I salute your courage."

With a wave of her hand, Louisa encouraged Nellie to go on.

"Well, I stood across the desk from Joseph and said, 'Go ahead. Send a man.' And I saw him relax. Then I said, 'And I'll do my trip for your competitor.'" All three of them laughed. "It was amazing to see him backpedal. 'Now, now, Miss Bly, let's not be hasty. . .' You know the kind of thing. That was a year ago, and finally, here I am.

"What route will you take?" The story entranced Louisa, as did its teller.

"America to England, then France, down to Brindisi in Italy, through the Suez Canal, touch base at Colombo in Ceylon and the Straits Settlements of Penang. Then, I will go to Singapore, Hong Kong, Japan, and the fastest ship I can get to San Francisco. I'll take a train from California through Chicago and back to Hoboken."

Louisa sat back, exhausted by the list of stops in the itinerary and the fact that each must be completed as quickly as possible.

"How did you prepare for such a monumental journey?" Ernest asked.

"I am traveling light," Nellie said proudly. "The dress you see me in is the one I will be wearing when I return to Hoboken. I have one bag for my papers, guides, and essential toiletries, and money in a pouch." She touched her chest where a slight bulge indicated its location. "With nothing I can't carry, I have nothing to wait for and nothing to care about except getting on to the next stop."

Louisa's eyes sparkled with respect. "Miss Bly, it's a wonderful undertaking, and I'm glad you're doing it. Not just as a human being but as a woman. Good for you. But," she looked into Nellie's eyes, "please do yourself the service of taking your eyes off the timetables and enjoying the journey. If I've learned one thing in my life, it's that the *going* is as important and fulfilling as the *arrival*."

Nellie's eyebrows rose as she considered Louisa's advice. "You're right, of course. And there will be inevitable pauses in the journey as I wait for connections. I promise to glean as much from each place as I can. Not only will it make it more fun, but it will also make for better articles—a better book—afterward."

Ernest glanced at his pocket watch and whispered to Louisa that perhaps she would like to move on to dinner. The three of them rose, and Nellie went to study the details for her first transfer.

~   ~   ~

November 25, 1889, London

Dearest Harriet:

I will send you letters of my adventures as I travel without concern for when (or even if) you will receive them. Writing to you helps me clarify my experiences.

When the ship arrived at Southampton, we saw our new friend, Nellie Bly, at the top of the gangway. She was first off the boat and disappeared quickly into the crowds, onto her next mode of transport. What an amazing young woman!

We were both right when we agreed Ernest would be an engaging companion on my journey. He introduced me to many fascinating people on the ship, including Miss Bly. He has a nose for characters. I did not have a dull moment or lonely meal the whole time at sea. He is also an able escort, dressing correctly for all occasions and facilitating things rather than leading them. I am so glad I didn't wait for an old stick!

London is grittier than I expected. Of course, some sections are lovely, and the public gardens are vast and beautiful. But in general, it is an old city that is feeling its years. We attended a public hearing at Parliament, which was most intriguing. Of course, Ernest managed to introduce me to some of the Members. I doubt you could put him down anywhere in a city and not watch him become friendly with the natives high and low within a day.

We are intentionally keeping our visit to England short to get on to France and beyond. Ernest has family roots in the Normandy area, and I understand the Sassevilles still have a home there. It will be interesting to see him interact with them.

I am looking forward to Paris, of course, and Ernest has assured me he will get me to the top of the Eiffel Tower. I have my doubts about that. But I long to taste the dishes I've read so much about in my guidebooks, sit in a cafe and watch people go by, and feel the rush and push of a city so foreign to any I have been in before.

I was worried I would not be able to stay away from home for a whole year. Now I wonder if I will even consider returning in less than two.

Affectionately,
Louisa

CHAPTER 21

November 30, 1889, France

Ernest smoothed his small mustache for the third time in less than five minutes as they rode across the fields of Normandy. Louisa noted the action. They'd made a most uncomfortable crossing from Dover to Calais three days previously and had been making their leisurely way southeast across France toward Sasseville.

"Are you nervous, Ernest?" Louisa cocked her head, intrigued to see him ruffled for the first time in their acquaintance.

He stared out the window of the motor car. "I would not call it nervousness. It is the uncertainty of my reception."

"But this is your family."

He gave her a wry grin. "And we both know how unpredictable family can be."

She nodded in agreement. "But do you expect them not to wish to see you?"

"You must understand, Miss Hovey. My family left this region many generations ago. Indeed, the Sassevilles were among the founding families of Quebec in the 1600s. It is very possible these Sassevilles will not even acknowledge me. The French are very proud. Anyone who chooses to live anywhere but here is, as you say, second class."

"Well, we'll just make the best of it either way, shall we? If they welcome you, that would be wonderful. If they do not, it is a lovely area, and we can explore what is here before moving on to Paris."

She felt him relax next to her.

"Truly, I am in admiration of you, Miss Hovey. I was concerned that you would be embarrassed by me or discouraged if this did not go well. Instead, you turn my own words back on me and remind me that we are on an adventure. Sometimes, they take different turns than we expect, no?"

She patted his hand. "No fears, Ernest. Regardless of your family, we will have fun." She thought for a moment. "Would you rather we skipped them altogether?"

"Oh, Miss, that is not possible. My family would never forgive me if I did not go to Sasseville. And if I go that far and not introduce myself, that would be criminal."

"Well, the last thing I want to do is be a criminal," she said with a chuckle.

"Then we shall proceed as if we had every right to be here. Such a thought has gotten me into more than one interesting place in the past."

"Of that, I am quite certain, Ernest."

~   ~   ~

The small farming village circled a Norman-era church and bustled with trade. They stepped down from their hired car into the town's market day with sights and sounds to delight Louisa. Her eyes gleamed as two small girls herded an unruly flock of geese down the street. Buyers and sellers shouted price and counter-price even though they were mere inches from each other's ears.

Ernest walked into a nearby restaurant and began speaking with the proprietor. Louisa contented herself watching the swirl of colors and sounds of vibrant life all around her. When an old woman approached her and held out loaves of fragrant bread from a basket over her arm, Louisa was distressed that she could not communicate with her. She longed to taste the bread. Instead, she held up her hands and said, "*No Francais*," as Ernest had taught her. The woman sniffed and moved on.

Ernest returned to her side after several minutes of gesticulating conversation. "I have located the directions to my family's home. Come. I will tell our driver where to go."

They again entered the car, and a louder conversation ensued. At last, the driver sighed, shrugged, and put the vehicle into gear. They circled the village and again headed across the fields.

A large manor house came into view. To Louisa, it was like a painting: the white house with its ancient but well-tended thatched roof, fields spanning out from it on all sides, and numerous people coming and going with carts, donkeys, baskets, and other loads. The car stopped before the house, and they sat gazing at it. Ernest finally gripped the door handle and opened the door.

A small child—Louisa thought it was a boy, but its hair was long, and its face was dirty, so she could not be sure—ran up to them and began to ask questions in rapid-fire French. Ernest immediately lowered himself to the child's level and spoke to him seriously and with great patience. The child darted away.

"I believe we are about to be announced," Ernest said, rising back to his feet. "I see a certain resemblance to my uncle Pierre in that child's countenance. Amazing."

Several adults came out to the drive following the child, and the conversation began again. Louisa wondered how she'd ever considered traveling anywhere without speaking other languages. She mentally blessed Ernest for his skills and tried to hear even one word she recognized. Finally, she heard it.

"*Oui! Oui!*" the oldest man exclaimed as he grabbed Ernest's arms and planted repeated kisses on both of his cheeks. A connection had been made at last.

Each of the others repeated the process with Ernest. Then he turned to sweep his arm in her direction. More talking included her name, and suddenly, they descended upon her, too. There was more hugging and multiple kisses.

"They recognize me!" Ernest said in relief.

"So I see," Louisa said as another loud kiss landed on her cheek.

"They are delighted to meet me and even more to have you here, Miss Hovey. They would like us to come inside."

The rest of the afternoon was filled with smiles, excellent food, glasses of the family's own wine, bread, and sauces to dip it in, and lots of laughter. Though the talk all went over Louisa's head except when Ernest paused to translate for her, the warmth and genuine enthusiasm for the visit were evident.

As the sun began to sink, serious discussion started once again. Ernest held up his hands and shook his head though he smiled. The others seemed to implore him. At last, he turned to Louisa.

"They want us to stay with them tonight. I have explained that we do not want to put them out. I must confide to you, Miss Hovey, that we should go on our way. I do not want to take someone else's bed, and I know you would feel more comfortable in a hotel where you can relax."

"Quite right, Ernest. This has been a remarkable and lovely afternoon. Please convey my deep thanks to them for it and for inviting us. But I agree it would be better to leave on a high note and not drag out our visit." After a moment, she added, "If you like, you can always return here alone while we are in France. I would not mind if you do."

With the salve of a possible future visit from their far-traveling relative, the family reluctantly escorted them back to the car. The driver had enjoyed his day as well., Kitchen tidbits had been brought to him and enough wine to give him a sound nap. He shook himself and opened the door for them. After more kisses than she could count, Louisa was relieved to feel the car move off again.

"We will stay in a hotel tonight and take the train to Paris tomorrow," Ernest said with another wave out the window. Then he turned to her and took her hands in his. "I thank you most sincerely

137

for allowing me this momentary connection to my family, Miss Hovey. You didn't have to agree to it."

"Ernest, let's agree on one thing. This is an experience for both of us, not just me. We are companions, not employer and employee. I enjoyed today fully. Let's go have more adventures."

~ ~ ~

November 30, 1889, Paris

My Dear Harriet:

I have only one regret about Paris, and that is that we left home too late to attend the Paris World Fair. It closed a month before we arrived here and was undoubtedly spectacular. Even the remains of the Fair have been interesting, none so much as the Eiffel Tower.

Though he urged me to experience being at the top of the world's tallest structure, I had to decline Ernest's offer to escort me there. It is over 300 feet tall, and the only way to the top is by a winding staircase. Were I Ernest's age, I would have certainly attempted it. But at my age. . .

I have been thinking about my age more than I would like to admit, Harriet, mostly with resignation. It's one of the few things you can't change about your circumstances. When I turn 50 next year, I think I might feel a bit old. I have to ask myself why I waited so long to do things.

Why did I wait until 40 before I took a chance and moved to Denver? Why have I stayed in Denver so long and not explored more of the planet? What is there about people who get complacent and can't seem to move themselves along toward new experiences without an almighty push?

Well, I'm moving now! We plan to linger in Paris for Christmas and the New Year and then contemplate where to go next. I am determined to try everything physically within my power. I'm not going to come home with a bag of regrets. At this rate, I may not come home at all.

Contemplatively yours,
Louisa

CHAPTER 22

January 1891, Spain

If there was a castle, cathedral, fountain, or forest they had yet to visit throughout France, Germany, Austria, Switzerland, and Spain in the past year, Louisa would be hard-pressed to name it or work up the enthusiasm to go there. She leaned back in the upholstered chair on the veranda of her hotel, overlooking the sunbaked Spanish landscape, and sighed.

She and Ernest had traveled for two years and felt she had seen all she could absorb and then some. Maybe it was time to go home at last.

Ernest crossed the flagstones toward her, every line of his body exuding excitement. He never seemed to lose his taste for travel, but he was even more avid today than usual.

"Miss Hovey, I have such news! Wonderful news!" He bowed, and she gestured to the chair opposite her. He dropped into it as if he'd run a distance, as indeed he had.

"What news could possibly reach you here on such a lazy day?" He took a deep breath, set his hat on the chair next to him, and fixed her with his liquid brown eyes. "What if I were to tell you that an old friend of yours was nearby and that you could travel with her for the next two months?"

Louisa almost groaned. More travel. But Ernest was quivering in his enthusiasm. "What friend?"

"*Augusta Victoria!*" he crowed.

It took her a moment to place the name of the wonderful ship they sailed in across the Atlantic to begin their travels. When she did, she wondered if he, too, was leading up to saying it was time to go home.

"Ernest, we are nowhere near the route of the *Augusta Victoria*. Whatever are you on about?"

"Let me explain. The *Augusta Victoria* will dock at Gibraltar on January 28." He consulted a note he'd written and went on. "She will then resupply and take on passengers for a magical journey throughout the Mediterranean for two months. She will go to Genoa, Alexandria, Jaffa, Beirut, Constantinople, Piraeus, Malta, Palermo, Naples, Lisbon, and then deposit you back at Southampton once more."

Louisa blinked.

"All on the ship you so loved when we crossed the Atlantic. You would travel comfortably with hundreds of fellow travelers, many of whom will speak English to you."

Louisa blinked again. Ernest began to shift in his chair.

"Do you not like this idea, Miss Hovey?"

Finally, she exhaled and focused on Ernest once more. The idea of more travel had been almost too much for her a few minutes ago, but the thought of that beautiful ship carrying her all around the Mediterranean Sea was refreshing and appealing.

"Have you already booked our tickets?"

"No, my lady. I wanted to talk to you before I did so."

"Well, that's a first." She smiled.

"It is a matter of. . . money. The tickets, they are quite expensive. I did not want to commit your funds without your approval."

"How much?"

"A thousand dollars a ticket."

Louisa frowned slightly and made slow circles on the crisp tablecloth as she considered what he'd said. Finally, she looked up again."If we spent the next two months traveling around, staying in hotels, and moving from place to place, it would cost us quite a bit. Not that much, but then we would not be sailing on the best steamer in the world."

Ernest nodded.

"Go buy the tickets, Ernest. It's time for more experiences."

"Oh, Louisa! I knew you would do it." He rose, dashed off, returned to snatch his hat off the chair, and charged off again.

She watched him go, alight with excitement and plans, and pondered on the fact that he had just called her by her first name. A fond gleam came to her eyes, and she decided she liked it.

~   ~   ~

February 15, 1891
Aboard the Augusta Victoria

Dear Harriet:

I thought I was coming home, but I am at sea again. However, it's a different sea and a completely different journey.

That marvelous ship, Augusta Victoria, *is wintering in the Mediterranean, and I am happily ensconced in a suite on board. I never fully explored or appreciated the ship in our eight-day Atlantic crossing. Now, I have time to soak it in.*

We are traveling with 239 other passengers, mostly German, British, and American. I have many to talk to, and Ernest is fluent in German to smooth any difficulties there.

I wish you could see this floating palace. Opulent decorations, spacious public rooms, an abundance of light even inside the ship, and an unending flow of delicious meals make one never want to get off.

But we do get off. At each port of call, excursions allow us to explore new places and shop for souvenirs. I admit I have just sent back my fourth crate of keepsakes to Rebecca's home so she can put them aside for me for when I return.

This cruise has allowed me to see Alexandria in Egypt—where I rode a camel!--and we go to the Holy Land, Lebanon, Constantinople, Greece, Italy, and Portugal. I never dreamed I would go so far. The trip's conclusion will place us back on English soil, but I am not even thinking of that.

Ernest continually amazes me with his ability to see to my every comfort. Our relationship has softened over time with constant companionship. I enjoy his wit and humor, his exuberance, and his flexibility. Any chance I get to make him happy, I do so. He deserves it.

Tomorrow, I set my feet on the soil of the Holy Land. Will it feel different than anywhere else I have been?

Affectionately,
Louisa

~   ~   ~

The dining room buzzed with its usual conversations, and Louisa nodded to the many new friends she had made on board. A whoop drew her eyes to the table of Germans. They wore identical hats and were cheering on one of their comrades as he ate.

"Those Germans," Ernest smiled fondly. "I have learned they made a pact before they got on this ship that they would do three things together."

"What are they?"

"They will acquire the same travel hats," he said.

She nodded. At every port of call, they all bought hats.

"They will relish every meal to the full," he went on.

She rolled her eyes.

"And they will eat as many caviar rolls as humanly possible."

143

"Well, they accomplished all that in the first week. Goodness, what funny people."

Louisa dropped her posy of violets into her water glass to keep it fresh. Every evening, the line's director, Albert Ballin, presented each of the 67 ladies on board with such a posy. She found it charming. Her room had fresh flowers every day as well. Altogether, it was a most satisfactory way to travel, she thought.

Mr. Ballin rose from his table and lifted his glass. They were celebrating Wilhelm II's birthday tonight, and he led them in toasts to the emperor's health and rule. Then, the conversation returned to normal levels.

"That was quite a salute we received in Alexandria, wasn't it?" Ernest said. Many ports they entered had never seen a ship as grand as the *Augusta Victoria*, and people lined the docks to cheer. Gunned salutes rang out, and the passengers received royal treatment.

"It has been a most enjoyable part of our travel. Thank you for acting on the information when you heard the ship would be at Gibraltar. I would not have missed this for anything," Louisa sipped her wine and gazed at the vast ceiling of the dining room with its colored glass and decorations.

Suddenly, she decided to broach a subject she'd been avoiding. "You've given up so much time and put great effort into this trip, Ernest. What about your own life? You've put yourself in a box and let life go by you while you accompany me hither and yon. Don't you long to go back to your own pursuits? Find a wife, settle down, have children."

Ernest thought for several seconds. He took a sip of wine and blotted his mustache with his napkin. "Louisa, I feel like I was just waiting for my life to start when I lived in Denver. I have seen many places these last two years, had experiences, and met interesting people. It's like I am finally living. You have not caused me to go into a box, as you say. You took me out of my box. I am most grateful."

"I would like to think that you are not just grateful to me but that you like traveling together. We've gotten past 'Miss Hovey'; can't we get past your feeling that you are one step behind me?"

A swell of singing from the German table gave Ernest a chance to formulate his reply. He turned back to face her fully and touched his heart as he spoke. "I do not feel I am beneath or behind you. If I behave that way, it is to protect you and your reputation, dear lady. Even here, so far from home, there are people among the guests who watch you, who may even report on you in letters home. I never want it said that I did anything to compromise your standing."

Now, it was Louisa's turn to pause and collect her thoughts. "I understand, Ernest. And I am grateful. I don't care what they write about me, but your generosity makes me very glad you put yourself forward as my best possible companion. You make me quite happy."

They lifted their glasses and touched them together, then sat back and watched the Germans.

CHAPTER 23

Summer 1891, London

Dear Louise-Caroline,

I trust you and the rest of the family are well. I am writing to you because I doubt Charles would read my letter. His continuing attitude toward me is hurtful, but it hurts him more than me. I regret that it hurts you as well.

In the past two and a half years, I have been to many places, seen many grand things, and experienced the wonder and beauty of different cultures. There have been many occasions when I wished to share this with others who would appreciate it. And it is with this in mind that I write to you.

Your daughters would benefit from a trip to Europe. At the very least, I could outfit them for a bright future. Though I love to look at the fashions in Paris and elsewhere, there are better models than me to wear them. As they say of large ships, my lines could be more pleasing. But Rebecca and Edith are young and attractive. They would be so fun to dress up and send home with a complete trousseau.

Edith is also an excellent musician. Words cannot convey the glory of sitting in a vaulted opera house in Vienna to listen to a choir and orchestra or hearing a master violinist play in Venice. Studying there would enhance her musical education.

Please ask Charles if he would allow me to treat them this way. Surely, he cannot feel that this would not be an experience well spent.

Think about it,
Louisa

September, 1891, Boston

Dear Louisa,

I thank you for your very generous offer regarding Rebecca and Edith. The truth is that life has moved on while you have been away. Our Rebecca is to be married later this month to George Fernald Reed. She will make a lovely bride. Of course, she cannot possibly travel anywhere with the wedding so near. I must decline on her behalf.

Edith is not attached, but there is another issue. I must be blunt, Louisa, and I pray you will not take offense. I will not approach Charles with this offer because I know he would be enraged by the idea. You see, we've had news from overseas while you are traveling.

A dear friend sent an issue of the little newspaper published onboard the Augusta Victoria. It included photographs and drawings of the passengers enjoying their various pursuits. I'm afraid there was one of you and your escort. It is apparent from that photograph that he is quite young. We were under the impression he was an older gentleman.

Oh, Louisa! What were you thinking to take a young, unmarried man with you all over Europe for years? The scandal has spread across Boston. Charles is ashamed, and no one dares to raise the subject with him. In no way would it be acceptable to Charles or me for Edith to join the two of you and continue your travels.

Edith is now nearly 23 years old and has no prospects of marriage like her sister. Any hint of scandal would permanently put marriage to a respectable man beyond her reach. As much as you wish to improve and bless her with your generosity, you would destroy her as a young woman.

Please understand,
Louise-Caroline

The cloud that clung to Louisa drifted until it enveloped Ernest as well. His typically sunny disposition evaporated in the face of her evident turmoil. Not knowing the cause of it, he did his best to amuse her and distract her with activities and light talk. Nothing worked.

As she lingered in the window seat of the house they were renting, Louisa sighed for the fourth time, gazing out at the unending London rain. Ernest could stand it no longer. He approached and sat down across from her on the seat.

"Louisa, what is it? You have been moping for weeks. Are you tired of travel? Do you want to go home? I thought you were enjoying the society here in London." He stopped and watched her. "Or is it me you have tired of?"

Louisa raised her eyes and studied his face. It was a good face—a kind face—one that made getting up in the morning something that she looked forward to and didn't dread. He was always there, always fun, always interesting. And that was the problem.

"Oh, Ernest. I am not tired of you. Never fear that. Tired of traveling? Perhaps. Ready to go home? I'm not sure about that. But I am sad. I wanted to bring my nieces to Europe and show them the best parts of what we have seen and experienced. But my family objects."

"They do not wish them to see these things?"

"They don't object to Europe. They object to you, Ernest. To us." Her head dropped forward and she raised a hand to her brow.

"But we have done nothing wrong. What is there to object to?"

She sighed. "In Boston, there is always something to object to. That is why I left it behind when I moved to Denver. Word has gotten back as you predicted, and they realize they erred when they thought my chaperone all this time was not an old man. Instead, he is young, attractive, and vibrant. He is you."

"I still do not understand. Am I so objectionable?"

"Not to me. Not at all. But the fact that you are young and unmarried means they will never send my niece Edith to visit. They fear more scandal even if it has no factual basis."

They sat quietly, listening to the raindrops tick against the glass. The fire in the fireplace did little to beat back the darkness of the day or Louisa's mood. Ernest had no idea how to help her, so he did what the English had taught him to do: he rang for some tea.

When the tea arrived, he poured hers, mixing the right amount of cream and sugar. He brought it to her in the window seat. She sipped it, then drank it as if she had made a decision. She put the cup down with a smart clack on its saucer.

"Ernest, there's only one thing to do. Will you marry me?" Ernest sputtered over his tea and coughed as some caught in his throat. When he could breathe again, he gaped at her. "Excuse me?"

She eyed him steadily. "Marry me. It's the perfect solution. It puts out the fire of scandal, paves the way for Edith to come, and would make me very happy. I would never be anything to you except a loving and generous wife eager to see you enjoy your life."

Her full face took on a ruddy glow. "I would not expect you to be a husband in the most intimate manner toward me. I am nearly old enough to be your mother. I am beyond the age when that appeals to me or is of any practical use. But we get along so well, Ernest. We've shared so much. I would be generous to you," she repeated.

Ernest set down his tea. "Louisa, it is traditional for the gentleman to ask the lady to marry him. But we have not had a traditional life these past years, have we? I began this journey as an excellent way to travel in style. But I have come to be very fond of you. If I had any idea you would even consider it, I would have proposed marriage to you. I want you to know that."

"But will you do it? Can we clarify this and return home as Mr. and Mrs. Sasseville?"

Ernest crossed one arm over his chest and brought his other hand to his mustache. He stroked it in thought as the mantle clock seemed to increase in volume, ticking off the moments. He stood abruptly, and she feared the worst. He moved to her side and took her hand.

"I accept, Louisa. If you first consent to be my wife, I will be your husband."

~ ~ ~

TELEGRAM

November 14, 1891

TO: LOUISE-CAROLINE HOVEY

I MARRIED ERNEST IN LONDON A WEEK AGO [stop] **PUT EDITH ON THE FIRST FEASIBLE SHIP IN THE SPRING AND CABLE DETAILS** [stop] **LOUISA HOVEY SASSEVILLE**

~ ~ ~

April 1892, Boston

"For the last time, absolutely not. And that is final."

"Charles Hovey, I am not taking no for an answer—not this time. I have taken it and taken it, and I am done taking it. This is about Edith, not you."

Charles rounded on Louise-Caroline. "You will listen, and you will obey me!"

She shook her head, and her greying curls danced. "When you chose our wedding date, I went along with it. When you chose the names of our children, I agreed. When you banished your sister from our home—albeit after she'd already left—I let you. When you made me cut off all communication with her, I did it. But not this time!"

"No daughter of mine is going to be tainted with scandal!"

Louise-Caroline rested a hand on Charles' rigid arm. "There is no more scandal, Charles. Our daughter is going to Europe for the trip of a lifetime with her married aunt and her husband. People do that all the time." She crossed her arms and took a step back from him. "Edith is 23 years old. She is unmarried. She has no prospects. Do you want her to sit in this house and grow old rather than grab this opportunity?"

Charles turned his back to her. She poked him firmly in the shoulder.

"You are so consumed with your dignity! I won't let you deny her this chance because of it. You only have one thing to decide."

He spun around and glared at his wife. "And what is that?"

"Whether you accompany us to the ship to see her off or not."

CHAPTER 24

October, 1897, Denver

"I have a bone to pick with you, my dear." Melissa Hotchkiss entered Louisa's parlor and sat beside her old friend. "When I told you to travel and see the world, I did not mean you should disappear from Denver for years!"

Louisa laughed. "It was some of the best advice I ever received. You were right; there's so much to see, do, and learn. I'm afraid it's become our lifestyle. I've just applied for yet another open-ended passport, and we'll no doubt be off again early next year."

Melissa made a mocking growl as she removed her gloves and dropped them onto her lap. "I haven't even heard about your last trip yet! And you've not seen the glorious things I brought back from Scotland."

When the tea arrived, it had an exotic aroma, and small cakes made from rice and spices accompanied it. "I got used to this while studying Buddhism in Japan last year. It was a peaceful time I will treasure, though I'm not ready to walk away from my church."

"I saw Ernest's articles in that new magazine, *The National Geographic*, a few months ago. It said he was writing from Paris. Wasn't he with you in Japan?"

"Sometimes we travel together, and sometimes I develop a passion for something, and he returns to France to visit family and friends." She smiled to herself. "I must admit that the most interesting times are when we travel together. He gets me into the most unusual situations."

Melissa's eyebrows quirked. "Such as?" She took a bite of the rice cake and decided she liked it very much. It had a hint of honey and some earthy tones, setting off the tea perfectly.

Louisa thought for a moment. "We've been all around the world and seen things from the deserts of Arabia to the jungles of Ceylon, ridden in ships with enormous sails in China, and danced highland jigs in Scotland." She thought further, then nodded her head.

"Here's a perfect example. We were in Cambodia. You know where that is?"

Melissa nodded. "I've never been. Go on."

"Ernest wrote it up and sent the article to the *The Rocky Mountain News* a few years ago. You didn't read it?

"I was off to Russia that year."

"Normal tourists would visit temples and travel by ship up the rivers. But Ernest must go further. He managed an audience with the governor of the province we were in and somehow got permission for us to visit the ruins of Angkor—off limits to almost everybody. It was not an easy journey. We went by boat up a river and then a small bullock cart and finally had to scale high steps to even higher causeways to get there. But what a wonder it was with the tropical sunset behind it."

"He does seem to be a resourceful person," Melissa nodded.

"We toured the ruins, returned to the capital, and then moved on to Sargon. We arrived just as a water festival was going on. There were to be boat races and other events that promised to be lots of fun."

She took a sip of tea and gazed off, remembering the scents and sounds.

"We saw a barge along the pier, and several Europeans sat in gilded chairs on the deck. A table was draped with a wonderful

153

embroidered velvet cover. You know how I love embroidery! Ernest took my hand, and we went aboard. It turned out the others were invited guests, but no one asked us to get off."

She laughed sheepishly. "Keep in mind we were in our usual sturdy travel clothes. These people had dressed as if for a social engagement. I felt a bit out of place, I can tell you. Suddenly, there was a flourish of trumpets, and the governor stepped on board. Then another flourish, louder and longer, and the king himself stepped aboard!"

Melissa clapped her hand to her open mouth. "I can just imagine what you were thinking."

Louisa's smile was wry. "I was in favor of getting off immediately, but Ernest leaned over and said, 'We shall just have to make good use of our American cheek here," and we stayed. I assure you, it's the only time I have been wined and dined by royalty."

Both women laughed heartily.

He is forever getting us into things like that. He walks across the earth as if everyone will welcome him and deny him nothing," Louisa said.

"It seems it was a good match after all, then. I was somewhat worried when I read the notices of your marriage and realized who you had wed. I worried he was after your money."

"I never pretend, even to myself, that he married me for my looks. We traveled together in great style for two years before we became man and wife. He got very used to that lifestyle."

"You have taken steps to safeguard your fortune?"

"My investments continue to make gains. I have settled a certain amount of capital on Ernest, so he does not have to continually ask me for funds for his various projects. I put some land under his control so he could mortgage it to others for income. He is taken care of, and so am I."

"Did you lose much in the silver crash last year?"

Louisa shook her head. "I did invest in some of that, but you taught me well that land retains its value most of all. I still have

154

investments in various mines; however, I always come back to land."

"What about your name change?"

"Ernest did that last year. As his name suggests, he has roots in the Sasseville area of France, but the correct way to refer to people connected to that family is DeSasseville. I suspect his ancestors, who emigrated to Quebec hundreds of years ago, were humble folk and did not want to put on airs. Ernest prefers it, though, so he had the court change it."

"He has risen far from delivering groceries to your back door." Melissa paused as Ingrid knocked on the door and brought a silver tray with letters. She set it on the table at Louisa's elbow, replaced the teapot with a fresh one, and left them.

As Melissa refreshed her cup of tea, Louisa leafed through the letters. Her eyes lit up when she saw one particular one.

"Here is something from Ernest," she said, unfolding the letter. "Perhaps it is word on when he will return from France. Surely, he'll be home before Christmas."

Her grey eyes moved briskly across the page, then suddenly stopped. She moved back and reread the paragraph she'd begun, and Melissa watched as all color left her broad face.

Louisa seemed to shrink. Her friend jumped from her chair and moved quickly to her side.

"What is it? What's wrong?"

Louisa kept reading, raising one hand to forestall Melissa's questions. When she'd finished, her fingers lost their grip, and the pages fell to the beautiful Turkish carpet at her feet.

Her throat worked. Finally, she said, "Ernest is in trouble. I need to go to him at once."

"But what is it? Is he ill? Has there been an accident?" Louisa got to her feet with effort and staggered to the door. Melissa watched her go and then bent to retrieve the letter.

She read only the first few lines. They were enough.

My dear Louisa,

I regret to write to you that I am facing a great trial. I have no way to cushion this blow to you, so I will write it straight out. A young girl has accused me of fathering her child, and she is suing me for support. . .

"Oh, Louisa!," she whispered.

CHAPTER 25

October 1897, Paris

S he did not remember packing her bags or the headlong trip across America. The sea crossing was interminable. Another letter from Ernest greeted her arrival in Paris, written after he knew where she would be staying. It gave scant details to soothe her heart. She responded immediately.

My Ernest,

I have arrived in Paris and am ready to render any aid you require to resolve your situation successfully. I assume you have an attorney, but I will gladly hire another if it would help.

What can you tell me about this young woman who accuses you falsely of this terrible thing? What is her motive? How can we persuade her to withdraw her complaint?

I am beside myself with concern for you. To be abroad, alone, and have to face such a thing. There is nothing I will not do to bring you safely home again. Please give me further information so that I may act on your behalf.

With love,
Louisa

Days elapsed while she waited for the outcome of the situation. The woman's name was Josephine Trombetta. He had indeed met her on his many trips to France. The more she heard, the more she realized she was giving him more credit than he deserved. There was something to this story.

Dear Ernest,

We have always been honest with each other, at least on my part. I always assumed you were as well. But there is something here that I need help understanding and can't quite bring into focus. I appeal to you as your wife and the greatest friend you will ever have to give me the full details of this story.

You may be reluctant to do so and afraid I will be angry. Nothing could be more hurtful than the uncertainty I suffer now. I have always labored to show you more kindness, love, and generosity than I believe any woman in the world has or ever will. It is for this reason that I desire to hear everything from you. You have withheld yourself from coming to see me. I can only assume this is due to fear of punishment. If this is the case, I can only say you do not know me.

Others have told me there is a basis for this lawsuit and that you are at fault. I feel foolish staying on in Paris if you have transferred your affections to another. If you do not come to me, I shall return home. Let me hear from you.

Lovingly,
Louisa

November 2, 1897

My Dear Louisa:

Your dear, kind and loving letter came to hand this morning and I hasten to answer. You have certainly heaped coals of fire on my head and made me ashamed of myself for having treated you as I did. You are quite right in saying that I do not know you. I did not half know and certainly failed to appreciate you as you deserve. I always held you in highest esteem as a thoroughly true and noble woman, but you have shown yourself even far ahead of my estimate.

I am quite satisfied that what you say is the truth when you say that no one in the world cares as much for me and would do as much to make me happy as you do or would do. I am satisfied that you are the only woman in the world who has loved me unselfishly or undeservedly. I shall never be loved by anybody as you have loved me, and I know I shall never meet a truer and stauncher friend than you have been.

If I only had your firmness, your nobility of character and your straightforwardness it would have kept me from many reckless actions which have brought sorrow to others. Alas! my weakness and my fickleness have been the cause of much trouble to myself and others. Since you have been so kind and good I will further confess and tell you all and show you how bad and deceitful I have been, and how unworthy I am of the love and esteem of so good a woman as you are.

Within the last two years, that is, while we were in Germany I was unfaithful to you and had intimate relation with a young girl who happened to be visiting at a house where I called quite often. Nobody knew that I was married and I was received by the family. I took advantage of that fact and flirted with that girl and we became quite intimate. So you see I have been unfaithful to you and brought trouble and dishonor on that family which is a very good and respectable one.

159

The girl knows now that I am married but the parents do not know it. I hope they never will. You see now that I am not worthy of your love and can hardly even look you in the face again. If I had known you then as I know you now things might have been different, but I did not dare tell you anything. Why do you rush right back to America? Why not wait awhile? I shall be here for few days longer.

Your very bad boy,
Ernest

Louisa wept as she read Ernest's letter. To know that this affair had gone on for a prolonged time, that the girl had produced a child, and that her family had no idea that Ernest was married when he pretended to marry the girl drew her sympathy for them. But for herself?

Hurt. Disillusionment. An ache of loneliness that she knew would follow her for the rest of her life.

She wondered at his amazement she would return to America without him. What did he expect her to do--invite his other family to dinner? She booked her passage home the same day.

If there was one thing she'd learned from Ernest, it was efficient travel organization.

~   ~   ~

Rocky Mountain News (Daily)
Volume 39, Number 9

January 9, 1898

DIVORCE IN THE HIGH LIFE

Madame L.H. De Sasseville Loses
Money and a Husband's Care

Illustrious French Name Dragged
in the Mire of a Divorce Court

Ernest De Sasseville Alleged to Have Made Away
with $35,000 Given Him to "Make a Good
Appearance" and to Have Tired of His Wife.

Suit for an absolute separation and alimony has been brought in the district court against M. Ernest de Sasseville by his wife, Louise Hovey de Sasseville. An injunction has been granted which restrains the husband from interfering with any of his possessions in Denver, aggregating $35,000 in value, until his wife proves that the big batch of securities now lying in the Colorado National Bank belong to her, and that M. De Sasseville has been guilty of the unauthorized handling of several thousand dollars of her money.

The principle charge in the complaint is infidelity and there are said to be many co-respondents, among them Mlle. Josephine Trombetta, with whom the husband is now claimed to be living in Geneva, Switzerland.

The institution of the proceedings by Mme. De Sasseville a few days ago has been studiously kept from the public. Both parties are well known in Denver, especially the plaintiff, who owns considerable city property and moves in wealthy society circles. From her statement of grievances against the monsieur, which was drafted by Attorney J.H. Pershing, the husband has evidently been hard up at times, as she put up the cold cash for them to travel abroad on, and placed an elegant home in Arlington Heights in his name, in order to "add to his standing in the community."

The husband will probably not know of the suit for several months, as service of the summons will be by publication in an Arapahoe county paper. . . .

CHAPTER 26

February 5, 1898, Denver

Dear Harriet:

Never again will I read newspaper stories about scandalous happenings. In the last few months, I have learned two things: real people are behind those stories, and the information in the press is more inaccurate than true. Having suffered the indignities of this treatment myself, I now have complete sympathy for anyone else so heralded.

I do appreciate your kind letters of support and outrage on my behalf. Things here go from bad to worse. I had hoped to complete this divorce in a quiet and orderly manner without Ernest even being involved. He has, after all, admitted one of the key points of the indictment.

But as the cruel newspaper story described two days ago, "The husband, supposed to be in England, turned up bright and smiling in division III of the district court." You know how endearing Ernest's charm can be, and he turned all of it on the court and the jurors. Honestly, I despair of even having a fair consideration of the facts.

163

Ernest's attorney hinted to the newspaper that significant disclosures are to come, though I can't imagine what they could be. "The defense will be a revelation to the plaintiff," he said. "It will paralyze her."

I am not the "paralyzing" kind, so I think he has overestimated Ernest's hand. The entire suit comes down to two things. First, that Ernest has been (and admitted to being) unfaithful for a prolonged period. Indeed, the young woman believed she was married to him and that their child was legitimate.

The second side is the tedious financial details. I put property and funds in Ernest's name to help him raise his credibility in the community. He allegedly turned around, reinvested the funds, and left my name completely off any deeds or accounts. It is a substantial sum, and this cannot stand.

I find each revelation of Ernest's behavior painful. If there was ever a woman who did all she could to lay the world at a man's feet, it was me. If it was "just" another woman, I could forgive and try to forget. If it was just the money, I could convince myself he made an error in judgment. But when one thing after another becomes public, I can only wonder, mostly at myself. It's hard to be this age and so rueful.

I wish you were here,
Louisa

The Rocky Mountain Times
February 20, 1898

DE SASSEVILLE DIFFICULTIES

New Complaints and
Replies of Salacious
Nature Before Court

164

Monsieur Desires Madame to Pay to Him Golden Alimony

Judge Palmer Asked to Enjoin the Wife From Disposing of Her Property Pending Adjudication of the Case – Bank Wants to Withdraw

----

The further it progresses in the courts the more scandalous does the de Sasseville divorce case grow. Yesterday morning the wife, Louise Hovey de Sasseville, filed an amended complaint embracing additional charges on actions learned of since the presentation of the first complaints, while the husband filed his reply thereto. The wife reiterates all of the accusations made several weeks ago and which were published at the time, and supplements them with others more scandalous in nature. She names Josephine Trombetta, Joanna Johnson and Anna Linder co-respondents.

Mme. De Sasseville charges that her husband was on trial in Munich on a criminal charge, and that the court records will show that he was declared to be the father of a child born to Anna Linder.

Henry Van Schaack filed the husband's reply containing allegations heretofore published. In addition, the answer says that the claims regarding Anna Linder are false; that the woman is bad and has an illigitimate child 7 years of age. He explains that he and his wife had separate accounts at the bank and individual holdings. He met her, he says, in 1889, and by her "blandishments and allurements" traveled with her through Egypt, Europe and Palestine. He married her by her "continued art, cunning and persuasion" in London, November 7, 1891. The husband claims that the madame has refused to bear him a child and that this is one of the grounds for asking for a divorce from her. The interesting part of the answer is the request that she be made to pay him alimony. . .

~   ~   ~

March 2, 1898, Denver

"I appreciate your prompt arrival to meet with me, Mr. De Sasseville. As you will hear, we have much to discuss."

Ernest stroked his mustache and settled into the leather armchair before his attorney's wide desk in the book-lined office on Capitol Hill. "You said it was urgent, and it was to my benefit. Please, Mr. Van Schaack, let us get down to business."

166

"I have received a package of documents from Mrs. De Sasseville's attorney, including a letter he directed me to deliver to you personally before I begin reading the other documents."

He handed across a sealed letter which Ernest took. He examined the handwriting and recognized it as Louisa's. He opened it slowly.

March 1, 1898

My dear Ernest,

I can only believe that you are as sick at heart as I am by the things being written about us in the press and stated in the open courtroom. Our next scheduled hearing is on March 3, and I implore you to think very hard about how this should progress. We have known each other for nearly a decade, my dear. I know you do not have it in your heart to say the cruel things alleged in the pleadings. I can only assume that your attorney has included language meant to evoke sympathy in court, even if it shades the truth beyond breaking. I believe your heart is tired, as is mine.

If ever you felt any affection for me or even fondness, I ask that you think back on the wonderful times we had all around the globe– the adventures, the moments of astonishment, the joy–and accept the offer I have put forward. I have to tell you that my attorney has tried to dissuade me from it and feels that to continue the trial would be to come out completely vindicated in the eyes of the law. But I have insisted on this course.

I will ever think of you with your enthusiasm boiling for a new expedition and your beautiful phrases that could pull me out of any down moment. I only ask that you use one of those phrases now and agree.

Still your wife,
Louisa

The lawyer looked over his glasses at his client. "Well? What does she say?"

Ernest folded the letter carefully and put it in his jacket pocket. "This is correspondence between a man and his wife. It is private."

"Mr. De Sasseville, I am your attorney. You are in the midst of a divorce. All correspondence concerns me, and I must know its contents."

Ernest thought for a moment. He looked out the window and saw a hawk floating far up in the sky out over the plains, circling free. He counted his heartbeats for several seconds. "All but this one. Please tell me what the documents say."

The attorney quivered with curiosity and indignation. But he could sense when his client was beyond pushing and relented. "Do you want me to read all the verbiage? They are quite lengthy."

"No, just tell me the final information."

"It is a trade. You will admit in court that you are guilty of all the allegations she has brought against you. You will return any real property she gave you. You also cease to fight the divorce." He paused, waiting for an explosion. None came. Ernest waved his hand to ask him to continue.

"In return, you will receive $5,000 free and clear, and you will leave the country." The lawyer glanced at one of the documents. "She does not say for how long, so that is apparently up to you. But you get the point."

Ernest examined his finely manicured nails. He watched the hawk again as it quickly dived toward the ground but came up with empty claws. He saw a dust devil stir in the dirt and dissipate.

"As your attorney, I must advise you not to accept this settlement. Clearly, she is worried you will keep everything you have, and she will have to pay you alimony for years to come." Van Schaack sniffed and made a sour face. "We will win this."

Finally, Ernest looked again at the lawyer and nodded. "Yes. I will win. I'm afraid you will lose, however. I will accept the offer."

"You can't do that! We have great sympathy among the men on the jury. This offer is nothing less than a bribe. You will give up a lifetime of wealth for what seems like a large amount right now."

A tiny smile crossed Ernest's face. "For the love of a woman whose heart is pure, whose impulses are unselfish, and whose kindness knows no bounds, I accept this offer."

He rose, picked up his hat, and left the lawyer gaping.

~　~　~

The Rocky Mountain Times
March 4, 1898

CONFESSIONS OF
A FRENCH ROUE

Serve to Give Madame
de Sasseville an
Absolute Decree

Resumes Her Name of Louise
Hovey and Holds Property
Worth $47,000

Husband Now En Route to Paris,
Where He Has Another Wife
and Child Importuning
Him for Means of Support.

The de Sasseville divorce case came up in Judge Palmer's division yesterday afternoon and the madame was duly divorced from her boy husband in exactly ten seconds after the jury had the matter in hand. . . .

. . . the court said: "Gentlemen of the jury, I have but one instruction to give you, and that is that you return a verdict for the plaintiff."

The foreman signed the document and Mme. Louise de Sasseville became Louise Hovey. All litigation over the property is over, and the "widow" comes out ahead with $47,000 in realty in her name. . . .

CHAPTER 27

November 1898, Denver

"If there is no other business for us to discuss, I will adjourn this meeting." Louisa let her eyes settle on each of the women of the Unity Ladies' Aid Society to allow them to speak. None did. She rapped her gavel on the table, and they all rose.

Chatter about the upcoming Christmas sale still consumed them. Louisa stood more slowly. As she continued to recover from the blow of the divorce, she felt her age in ways she never had before.

At fifty-eight, she sought to put her practical mind and willingness to assist others to good use through Unity Church, to which she belonged. At least the gossips had stopped leaving their cards at her door. She was never "at home" to them.

It was fulfilling to feel needed again. The church ladies had made her the society's president and depended on her for advice and organization. This Christmas sale promised to be the most successful to date, with fancy work, candy, embroidery, and appropriate Christmas items available.

As she entered her rented home an hour later, she looked around with a frown. It was a beautiful home in the Capitol Hill district with tall white pillars out front and plenty of space inside, but it was not hers. Perhaps it was time she gave up her vagabond life and put down permanent roots.

The many treasures she'd brought back or sent home from her travels deserved a place to be displayed properly. For now, many of them languished in trunks and crates in storage rooms on the second floor. It was time she made a personal land purchase and built a house to meet her specifications.

She nodded decisively and headed for her desk in the parlor, pausing briefly to ring for a pot of tea. There was a great deal of planning to do.

~   ~   ~

November 20, 1899, Denver

Dear Harriet,

I am just home from the annual meeting of the Unitarian Society and its dinner. I am pleased that I was re-elected to the board. I firmly believe this is not just because of my money but because I have a logical mind and can get things done. (Confidentially, I treat them all like ten-year-old boys, and they respond to my authority.)

It also indicates that the whole scandal last year and its aftermath this year are behind me. It has been a very long and painful road, my friend. For months after the decree, I stopped going about in society. Did I ever tell you that Ernest attended a prominent tea party only three days after the court hearing? I worried he would continue his charm offensive, but he left the country shortly after that. It was a relief. I have not kept track of him since then.

This year, I have slowly eased back into attending various quiet events, mostly with Unity Church or going to the homes of close friends. New scandals have erupted here in Denver, and those who hounded me to tell them all the details of mine have moved on. Fame may be fickle, but true infamy still takes a while to go away.

The builders have nearly finished the house, and I anticipate moving in at the beginning of the year. I'm delighted I bought two lots instead of just one. You know how I love to sit in the garden, and this will have plenty of room for one. I have also made every effort to build a modern house. It has 12 rooms, a reception hall, two bathrooms, a hot water heating plant, and electricity. It will be the last place I live, so I want it to be comfortable.

Most of all, I can spread out my treasures and spend time reliving the best parts of my life. Each carpet, every curio, all my embroideries and pottery, and the brass chandelier that will hang in the entry hall all remind me of the moments of discovery in distant lands. Fortunately, my mind can separate the good times from those that came after.

One thing that will go straight to the attic, however, is my collection of trunks and suitcases. My traveling days are well and truly over. I can't think of anything I'd still like to see, and the idea of hiring a new concierge to escort me fills me with horror. My hearth and home will be my sanctuary.

I wish you could come for another visit, but I understand entirely the physical restrictions you suffer. None of us genuinely appreciate this business of getting old until we suddenly find ourselves past the point of no return. But we're still breathing, so all is not lost. Take care of yourself.

Affectionately,
Louisa

~   ~   ~

TELEGRAM

May 11, 1900
TO: LOUISE HOVEY DE SASSEVILLE

CHARLES DIED TODAY [stop] **AT LEAST HIS YEAR OF ILLNESS IS OVER** [stop] **FUNERAL WILL TAKE PLACE THE DAY AFTER TOMORROW IN BOSTON** [stop] **LOUISE-CAROLINE HOVEY**

~ ~ ~

Louisa carefully put the copy of the telegram into her writing case. She wanted to think for a few days before writing Louise-Caroline. Though his death was not a surprise, the timing of it was.

It made her feel odd to think the shadow of her half-brother's disapproval had dissipated with his passing. She couldn't honestly say she would miss him and his censure of her. She only regretted they had never come to an understanding. At least she was free to communicate with Louise-Caroline once again.

She moved through the rooms of her lovely home, straightening a painting here and touching a fine piece of embroidery there. The oriental carpets set off everything magnificently. White lace curtains at the windows and mahogany or birds-eye maple furniture throughout made her proud to invite friends to see her collections.

After a time, she settled into her comfortable wing-backed chair and picked up the most recent book she had been reading. *Paola and Francesco* began as a love story but quickly moved to tragedy, betrayal, and the consequences of poor choices. She sighed. *I've been reading all too much of this kind of thing lately.* She vowed to move on to more edifying reading--as soon as she finished the book.

Her shelves groaned under the weight of travel books, stories of train robberies and life on a ranch in Wyoming, a complete set of her beloved Dickens bound in leather and with gilded pages, French grammar books, world history books, and novels of every description. She had read constantly during her travels but left those books behind in exotic places rather than carrying them home. Her collection was growing nicely once again.

174

Her eyes drooped, and the book slid softly from her hands to her lap. Louisa moved back and forth through her life in dreams full of color and sensation. When Ingrid came to check on her mistress, she saw the gentle smile on her lips, silently retrieved the tea service, and left her to her unconscious wandering.

~   ~   ~

March 4, 1901, Denver

I, Louise Hovey de Sasseville (nee Louisa Jane Hovey), of the city of Denver, Arapahoe County, State of Colorado, being sixty years of age and of sound mind and disposing mind and memory, do make, publish and declare this, my last will and testament, in manner following. . .

FIRST: I will and direct that my body be cremated and that my funeral be conducted with as little pomp and ceremony as possible.

SECOND: I will and direct that my funeral expenses and all my just debts be paid out of my estate as soon as may be consistent with the proper and businesslike management of my estate.

THIRD: I give and bequeath to my sister, MRS. REBECCA F. SAMPSON of Roxbury, Mass., all of my embroideries, rugs, bric-a-brac (not, however including my cabinet and the contents thereof, consisting of curios, bric-a-brac, antiquities,

175

etc., collected during my travels), pictures, china and jewelry not herein otherwise disposed of. . .

FOURTH: I give and bequeath to my niece, EDITH HOLLIDAY, of Sharon, Mass., wife of Guy H. Holliday, my solitaire diamond ring, with pearl guard, and my collection of photographs, contained in albums, collected during my travels. . .

FIFTH: I give and bequeath to my niece, REBECCA F. REED, of Wellesley Hills, Mass., wife of George F. Reed, my diamond and sapphire ring and my diamond and ruby ring.

SIXTH: I give and bequeath to HELEN SAMPSON REED, daughter of the aforesaid Rebecca F. Reed, my gold watch and chain.

SEVENTH: I give and bequeath to my niece, JEAN E. HOVEY of New York city, N. Y., wife of Charles H. Hovey, junior my souvenir spoons, collected during my travels.

EIGHTH: I will and direct that my executor, hereinafter named, shall convert into money, as soon after my decease as the same can be done in a businesslike way and without loss or sacrifice, all of my estate, real, personal or mixed, of whatsoever kind or character and wheresoever situated, except what is herein otherwise specifically disposed of. . .

[Specific gifts, bequests and provisions]

A: To THE FIRST UNITARIAN SOCIETY OF DENVER, COLORADO, the sum of Fifteen Hundred Dollars ($1500). . .

B: My executor to pay over to the New England Trust Company. . . Five Thousand Dollars ($5,000) to be invested in the general trust fund of said Company for the benefit of LOUISE C. HOVEY of Boston, Mass. . . .

C: My executor to pay over to the New England Trust Company. . . Ten Thousand Dollars ($10,000) to be invested in the general trust fund of said Company for the benefit of HARRIET E. DAVENPORT of Roxbury, Mass. . . .

NINTH: I give, devise and bequeath to my nephew, CHARLES H. HOVEY, JUNIOR, commonly called "Carl Hovey" of New York City, N.Y., my niece EDITH HOLLIDAY of Sharon, Mass., wife of Guy H. Holliday, and my niece REBECCA F. REED of Wellesley Hills, Mass., wife of Charles F. Reed, their heirs and assigns forever, all the rest, residue and remainder of my estate. . . share and share alike.

TENTH: Other than those herein mentioned

there are no legal claimants to my estate and I recognize none.

ELEVENTH: I hereby nominate, constitute and appoint GUY H. HOLLIDAY of Sharon, Mass., and GEORGE F. REED of Wellesley Hills, Mass., to be joint executors of this, my last will and testament. . . .

CHAPTER 28

May 16, 1903, Denver

WITHOUT WARNING

**Mrs. Louise Hovey de Sasseville
Stricken Down by Death
While Alone In Her Room**

**She Was Well Known in Denver
Because of Her Philanthropic
Work – Married the Son of a
French Nobleman**

Louise Hovey de Sasseville was found
dead in bed at her home, 144 Sherman

Avenue, at 11 o'clock yesterday morning. The discovery was made by Mr. Davis, a neighbor and friend, who gained entrance to the sleeping apartment on the second floor means of a ladder. Dr. Buckley gives the cause of death as heart failure and says it occurred ten hours before the body was found.

Mrs. de Sasseville was descended from a Boston family of wealth and high station and was a woman of refinement and culture. It was she who obliterated the building debt of $3,000 on Unity Church and all outstanding obligations, being herself the principal contributor. She gave the church its fine pulpit and paid for the cement walks around the building. Her philanthropic spirit was manifested in many ways. She was a woman of means and generous purse, yet, withal was unostentatious.

She was the divorcee of Dr. Ernest de Sasseville, who is the son of a French nobleman. Count de Sasseville, of Normandy. The couple traveled abroad for years, visiting Europe and the Orient, and the home which Mrs. de Sasseville built at the southeast corner of Sherman and Second avenues is filled with foreign curios, many of them the finest to be found in America. Among the valuable of these is a hammered brass candelabra and a hanging lantern from Algiers.

Spent Evening With Friends.

Mr. and Mrs. de Sasseville came to Denver to reside, but domestic troubles arose and the wife sued for separation. After a long fight in the courts—the decree being contested by the husband—a divorce was granted, the wife retaining her husband's name. Mr. de* Sasseville subsequently entered Rush Medical College and has made a brilliant record in medicine. He is a fine linguist. His whereabouts could not be learned.

Friday evening Mrs. de Sasseville spent several hours with the Davis family next door, and Miss Davis spent the night with her. Yesterday morning Miss Davis returned home. Mrs. de Sasseville's Swedish maid, Ingrid, could not get into her mistress' room, and finally the neighbors became alarmed and forced an entrance. Mrs. de Sasseville seemed to be peacefully asleep, and the physician says she passed away suddenly in the midst of her slumbers. She seemed perfectly well the evening previous. At bed time she bade Miss Davis a cheery "good night and pleasant dreams." These were the last words she spoke. She was 63 years of age.

Her nearest relatives—who have been notified by wire of the sudden death—are Mrs George Sampson, her half-sister, residing in Boston, and her nephew, Carl Hovey of New York. No arrangements have been made for the funeral. A memorial service will be held in Unity Church as soon as Rev. David Utter returns from Boston.

~ ~ ~

May 23, 1903, Denver

The women gathered around their usual meeting table, but no one could look at the empty chair at the head of it. They put aside all thoughts of jumble sales and craft fairs as they tried to come to grips with the loss they had suffered.

"So I take it we agree that we need to submit something to the newspaper to commemorate her life and importance to us, correct?" asked Julia Petrie, now society's president. It had fallen to her to rally the Ladies' Aid Society.They nodded silently.

"Mrs. Utter, would you read the wording we have put together?" After clearing her throat, Rebecca Utter's clear voice reached across the room and spoke from their hearts.

"By the death of Mrs. De Sasseville this society has sustained a great and permanent loss. For many years her able leadership, her hearty co-operation and her generous support have been our reliance in every enterprise. The shock of her sudden removal brings a painful sense of personal loss to each one of us, and her name will always be held in grateful and affectionate remembrance. -- Julia C. Petrie, president; Rebecca P. Utter, secretary."

Julia raised her bowed head. "The paper has agreed to print this on its pages tomorrow. We should adjourn until next week as none of us is quite up to focusing on projects just now. Please remember that Pastor Utter is in Boston. Remember the kind gesture he has suggested we perform when he conducts the funeral later this week."

~ ~ ~

Boston Evening Transcript
May 26, 1903

Funeral of Louise Hovey de Sasseville

Simple funeral services were held at eleven o'clock this morning in the chapel at Mount auburn Cemetery for Louise Hovey de Sasseville who died at her home in Denver, Colo., on the sixteenth. Mrs. de Sasseville was formerly a resident of Boston, being a member of an old Boston family, but removed to Denver a number of years ago.

The services were conducted by Rev. David Utter of Denver, Mrs. de Sasseville's pastor as well as her personal friend. After the prayer and the reading of the scriptures, Dr. Utter referred to her simple life and mode of living as an inspiration and example to all with whom she came in contact and also said that while her friends here in the East were gathered to pay their last tribute at her funeral there were hundreds in that far Western city who mourned her death and were keeping account of the difference in time in order that they might think of this service here when it was observed. There was no music

Arranged around the chapel were potted palms and other plants while on the casket were strewn small clusters of pink and white roses, mingled with maidenhair fern. At the

close of the service in the chapel the body
was cremated.

~   ~   ~

June 7, 1903, Denver

Rebecca Utter straightened her husband's collar as he completed
his preparations for church. With a gentle finger, she smoothed the
small frown on his forehead.

"I know this will be a hard service, my dear. Have you made
your final choice of remarks you plan to make?"

Reverend Utter sighed deeply. "Yes, it's hard. The loss of Mrs.
de Sasseville still rings in my head every time I pass her home or try
to corral a committee meeting. There was nothing easy about her
role here in the congregation, but she made it look like it were."

With a final straightening of his shoulders and a nod to his
reflection in the mirror, he offered his wife his arm, and they turned
for the door.

When they arrived, the church was filling up with subdued
conversations, and many people wore sober black. He was glad
he'd had nearly a month to accustom himself to the fact that Louisa
would not be in her usual seat, but a lump rose in his throat when he
saw a band of purple ribbon enclosed her pew. Large clusters of
purple and white iris and snowballs decorated the solemn space.

Music and choral selections reflected her refined tastes and
quieted his heart. At last, he rose to pay tribute to a woman who
had, at turns, amused, baffled, and inspired him.

"We gather here today to remember the life of one of our
members, our good friend Louise Hovey de Sasseville. It would be
easy to focus on her impact on our church. She contributed so much
to liquidating the church debt when she challenged us all to pool
our resources and generously made up the difference of $3,000
from her purse."

He ran his hands over the smooth wood of the podium. "She gave us this pulpit and made many other contributions to our surroundings. Her tireless efforts with the Ladies' Aid Society and on our board helped make this congregation what it is today."

A brief smile blossomed on his face. "So very sincere and straightforward herself, it would have grieved her to think that after her death any extended eulogy or analysis of her character or account of her life should be spoken here or elsewhere. These wishes I shall respect. But I cannot let her leave-taking pass without saying that our sorrow is simply that she is gone, that her work here is ended and that we shall see her face no more."

The congregation gave quiet sniffs. He saw a man scribbling notes as he spoke and realized his words would be in the paper the next day. He blocked the thought and focused on Louisa.

"She died like another of our good friends, Mrs. Belden, a little more than a year ago—a simple, painless passage from sleep to death, without a moment's anticipation of the great change. We grieve not that she died suddenly, but that she died so soon. We are sorry that her work could not go on. There are never too many in the world who really care to do good, as she did, to be helpful to others, as she was.

"Our little world is poorer now that she is gone. Yet if we are brave and true there's nothing for us but to close up our ranks and march on when our companions fall. We doubtless leaned upon our friend too much. Let us replace an act of selfish sorrow with self-reliance and courage. Our friend left us a noble example; let us follow it. She learned how much better it is to live to be helpful to others than to see to one's own pleasure.

"The basis of Mrs. De Sasseville's many benefactions was her generosity, and in what she did through this disposition she found, I think, the most real joys of her life."

They sang Louisa's favorite hymn, and the congregation quietly left the sanctuary. Rev. Utter took one last look at the decorated empty pew. *Oh, Louisa! How we will miss you.*

185

EPILOGUE

Louisa's will designated her former student Guy Holliday, now married to her niece Edith Hovey, as one of her two executors. Her brother-in-law, George Sampson, was another. They faced the daunting task of probating a will from 2,000 miles away.

Guy traveled to Denver at once upon hearing of Louisa's death and, after hiring local attorney Carle Whitehead to oversee the probate process, escorted her body back to Boston for the funeral. They documented every step of the process in over 60 pages of inventories, court proceedings, receipts, and other reports to the court. No doubt it was more fuss than Louisa would ever have wanted.

Her total estate amounted to a million and a half dollars in today's money, despite the discovery of fraudulent dealings of thousands of dollars by some who owed her payments for land she generously mortgaged to them. These debts were declared "hopeless."

Paging through the inventories is like walking through her home. She had an eye for beautiful furniture. Every wall held paintings or other hangings from around the world. She loved glassware, lovely china, and pottery—that list runs to a page and a half all by itself. Jewelry, especially rings and broaches, was a passion as well. Dozens of fine embroideries were on display, whether done by her or others.

And books. Pages of the inventory list the title of every book found in the house. Though the names are not familiar in modern times, a quick Internet search shows the bent of her reading in the final years of her life and the depth of the pain she suffered in losing Ernest. Most of the books were published between 1898 and 1902. She must have left many books in her wake across the globe.

Her wardrobe was surprisingly modest, though of top quality. She had just a dozen dresses, with capes, coats, fans, shawls, and lace collars to vary them. She had 16 pairs of gloves and 22 handkerchiefs in lace, silk, and plain cotton. Thirteen black ostrich feathers were no doubt used to accessorize hats and bags.

Having traveled extensively in the Orient, Louisa dedicated an entire room to pieces she brought back. The Oriental Room was undoubtedly quite exotic to those who visited her. She also had a Pink Room, as that color seemed to bring her particular pleasure.

Everything in the house had to be accounted for, so a final miscellaneous category listed her various trunks and valises for travel, a lawn hose, a carpet sweeper, brass poles and rings for draperies, and one ton of coal.

Despite their meticulous work in reviewing Louisa's belongings, experts had to revalue many of her curios and antiquities in 1905. Her executors initially listed them at paltry prices of fifty cents or a dollar. Once transported to New York City and adequately examined, they added hundreds of thousands of dollars to her estate.

~   ~   ~

July 16, 1903, Denver

The flow of people passing through the doors of Louisa's home continued all day. A line had formed early, and darkness fell before it disbursed. Some came merely to look at the large house with its magnificent furniture and to gaze in wonder at the collections of antiquities and other souvenirs Louisa had accumulated. Others walked out with furniture, tapestries, china and pottery, books, and kitchen goods.

The sale brought in thousands of dollars. Buyers judged the prices fair but by no means equal to what had been invested in the goods. Louisa designated gifts from her heart for specific relatives and friends; these were carefully preserved and guarded in an upstairs room.

The next day, a news reporter described the home as "among the most handsomely furnished of the city, many of its embellishments being chosen by the most cultured taste in years of travel." The article went on to describe the heart of Louisa's treasured collection.

"Among the most highly prized collections of the entire property was one of scarabs, one of the most complete in the West. One very valuable specimen, which is claimed as the only one of its kind in existence, represents King Thotmes III overcoming his enemies in northern Syria. It is said that an agent for the British Museum tried to buy this scarab, but was only allowed to take a wax impression."

All marveled as they walked beneath the ornate Algerian antique brass lamp that hung in the reception hall. At Louisa's request, electric lights were added to it.

At the end of the day, the house echoed emptily, and the attorneys charged with distributing her belongings headed home, tired but content they had done their duty. Thus, the mementos of Louisa's life were scattered like ashes in the wind.

Author's Notes

People ask writers of historical fiction, "How much of this is true, and how much did you make up?" Novelists in this genre walk a fine line between sharing every detail of the information gleaned through years of research, and the need to tell a compelling and  coherent story. I hope I have walked that line well.

Research is like stringing a harp. Each fact, document, and newspaper article adds another rich string to the frame. The actual writing involves deciding which strings to pluck and which to leave alone to form a satisfying tune.

My interest in Louisa began after reading an article published in the January 1971 issue of *Yankee Magazine*. A family member wrote it, and the story has been a legend among us ever since.

The gist of the story was that Louisa, until then a traditional Boston school teacher, went West to see the Rocky Mountains and fell in love with them. At the train station, before she returned, she was approached by a swindler who talked her into buying a piece of land. He said the state Capitol would be built on it, and she'd make a lot of money. At the time, the plan was to place the Capitol in Golden, so he lied to her. However, the joke was on him because the legislature decided to put it in Denver and on her land! That transaction made her rich, and she traveled the world with her former grocery delivery man, Ernest Sasseville. He later betrayed her and she divorced him and died of a heart attack after climbing too many stairs when an elevator was not working to visit her lawyer and change her will.

It was a story designed to intrigue me, and I set out to find the backup documents behind it. I could prove practically *nothing* of the legend! However, the facts I uncovered were even more interesting, so the book was born.

I relied heavily on Ancestry.com, Newspapers.com, and various individual newspaper archives. I also followed the trail of any detail (such as the *Augusta Victoria,* or the life of Nellie Bly) to build a fuller picture of the times in which Louisa lived. I did not contradict anything that I found facts to substantiate. The newspaper articles I quoted in the book are authentic.

Dates and places are accurate to the best of my ability. I gleaned them from passport information, city directories, and other sources. Conversations and letters are my imaginings. The one exception is the long letter of confession Ernest wrote to Louisa, which was produced in court and quoted in the newspapers. I decided that if I could not prove something one way or the other, I had a license to invent the strings to tie the story together.

Louisa lived and breathed, as did Ernest. Charles Hovey and his wife Louise-Caroline Hovey, their daughters Edith Hovey Holliday (and her husband Guy Holliday) and Rebecca Frances Hovey Reed (and her husband George Fernald Reed) are all real. Charles Hovey Jr. (known as Carl) was real, and fulfilled my imagined approval by his uncle: his headstone in the family plot at Mt. Auburn reads, "Author and Editor." Louisa's half-sister Rebecca Frances Hovey Sampson, her publisher husband George Sampson, and Louisa's friend Harriet Davenport are real people.

Nellie Bly did, indeed, go around the world and made it in 72 days, thanks to some fudging by her editor in hiring a private train to race her back across America. Whether she and Louisa met is my fantasy.

I do not know to what lengths the family went to keep Louisa from moving to Denver. The scheme to have her committed is my invention. However, the story of Mrs. Packard is accurate. Many women in those days were placed in insane asylums for similar "crimes." In fact, Nellie Bly got her start as a journalist by posing as such a woman in a notorious asylum and writing a book about it—after her publisher intervened to get her out of the place.

Melissa Hotchkiss was an exciting find. After spending whole evenings online paging through land records from Denver between 1876 and 1886, I never found a single reference to Louisa Jane Hovey. However, Melissa's name came up over 150 times in land transactions. I have no evidence they ever met, as I couldn't find any other facts about Melissa anywhere. Therefore, I was free to invent their friendship. To my knowledge, Louisa never that particular deed to show her friends back in Boston.

I spent over 20 years researching Louisa's life. Each time I hit a wall, I put the project aside and returned when more resources became available online. When she was 80, my mother (Marcia Taylor Reed Miller Todd) said it would please her if I wrote something about Louisa. I finally finished the book in time to give it to her as a gift on her 100th birthday. I'm glad she never said *when* I needed to have it done. . .

The divorce of Louisa and Ernest was the equivalent of a tabloid sensation today. I found over 70 newspaper articles and references to various parts of the trial. Louisa's reactions to it all are my conjecture, but I do not think I am far off the mark, based on what I learned of her character.

And whatever became of Ernest?

I have to admit I fell in love with Ernest a bit myself, rogue that he was. My grandfather, Paul Spencer Reed, son of Rebecca Frances Hovey Reed, allegedly said of Ernest, "He was the most charming man I ever met." He certainly seemed to move through life in a way that confirmed that.

After the divorce, he left the country, as stipulated by Louisa's settlement with him. He later returned, apparently after changing his name again (to Ernest Max *Sasvil*, and later *Sasville*.) Whether he did it legally or not is unclear. People changed their names all the time in those days, and there were no computers to complain (just genealogists many decades afterward.) He used the money Louisa gave him (equivalent to about $100,000 in our dollars today) to go to Northwestern University Medical School in Evanston, IL. He graduated in 1902 as a doctor of osteopathy (chiropractic) and practiced from then until he died in 1939 to great success.

Ernest married again—twice. First, to Bess Hurlbert in December 1903. She gave him a daughter, Alice Lillian Sasville. Bess died in 1924, just a week after completing her chiropractic training at the famous Palmer School of Chiropractic in Iowa. Their daughter, who was just 17, vowed to attend the same school and take up the same profession.

Ernest's third wife was Mrs. Lucille Holt of Asheville, NC., whom he married in 1936, just three years before his death.

Ernest truly did send a lengthy travelogue home to *The Rocky Mountain News* from their tour through the Far East. He also wrote some articles for *The National Geographic* magazine after he met explorers when they returned to Europe in 1896. Those articles were included in the January 1897 issue. In this way, he continued his passion for travel through the exploits of others. In his later years, he gave lectures on subjects like "My Trip to the Holy Land."

On August 27, 1939, Ernest was attending a church camp near Waterloo, IA, when he died suddenly in his sleep of heart failure. Charming to the end, he was said to have entertained the gathering the evening before by singing songs in English, French, and German.

I have a few things that belonged to Louisa, and it inspired me to hold them in my hands. Louisa directed that a diamond and ruby ring should go to her niece, Rebecca Hovey Reed. She passed it down to her daughter-in-law, Bonnie Reed (my grandmother), who passed it to my mother. I enjoy having it circle my finger on special occasions. It fits nicely.

When the female family members split up my grandmother's china, one of Louisa's custom-ordered teacups and saucers was among her things. It had a unique design and her name was written on the bottom of it. I took it. If it didn't have a hairline crack in it, I would drink from it every day.

I clearly remember the treasured oriental rugs that graced the floors of my grandparents' home in Tulsa, OK. I would have given a great deal to get my hands on the 14 photo albums of images collected by Louisa during her extensive travels. What a treasure trove they would have been!

But what means the most to me is the time I have spent tracking Louisa's life through documents and newspaper accounts as I sought to get to know this remarkable woman. She was impulsive, yet practical. Her actions showed determination and imagination beyond her era. She was generous, pragmatic, optimistic, unconventional, and brave.

Louisa did not have children, but I'd like to think some of her spirit has come down the family line, even to me.

BeccaAnderson
Longview, Texas
June 21, 2024

About the Author

Becca Anderson has been a writer and editor for over 40 years. For the last 25, she has worked with her mother producing a Canadian trade magazine. Sporadically, she feels the siren call to write a book, despite learning the hard way that it will take far longer than she thinks, and be much more work than it should. But it will also be lots of fun.

She loves to hear from readers! You can email her at banderson@cablelynx.com.

Books by Becca Anderson

(Available on Amazon as paperbacks or ebooks)

Shadow of Deceit

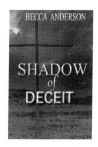

Casey Ellis is a Christian who wants more out of life, and out of her faith. She finds a church that seems to be exactly what she's been searching for. But when alarm bells begin to ring, she must find a way to escape and make her way back to solid faith again. (Previously published as *The Gathering Place,* by David C. Cook Publishing.)

Pushing Back the Darkness

The true story of Jennifer Redcay's experience with the darkest side of

194

spiritual deception. After reading *The Gathering Place*, Jen contacted Becca and told her an amazing story that put fiction to shame. Together, they set out to share her cautionary tale, from despair to triumph.

Oh, Louisa!

A historical novel based on the life of Becca's great, great, great aunt. Louisa Jane Hovey was born in 1840, and lived a conventional life in Boston as an old maid schoolteacher until the age of 40. Then she pulled up stakes, moved to Denver, made a fortune, traveled the world and married a most unusual man. The end of her life was anything but conventional.

Coming soon?

Having written a novel, a non-fiction book and a book of historical fiction, it's a complete mystery what she'll write next. . . .

Made in the USA
Middletown, DE
14 September 2024

60479336R00115